HER STORY

Other books by Dan Jacobson

Novels

The Trap
A Dance in the Sun
The Beginners
The Rape of Tamar
The Wonder-Worker
The Confessions of Josef Baisz
The Price of Diamonds

Stories

Through the Wilderness: Selected Stories

Autobiography

Time and Time Again

Criticism

The Story of the Stories

Dan Jacobson

HER STORY

A NOVEL

ANDRE DEUTSCH

First published 1987 by
André Deutsch Limited
105-106 Great Russell Street London WC1B 3LJ

British Library Cataloguing in Publication Data

Jacobson, Dan
  Her story.
  I. Title
  823'.914[F]   PR6060.A3

  ISBN 0–233–98116–0

Phototypeset by Falcon Graphic Art Ltd
Wallington, Surrey
Printed in Great Britain by
Ebenezer Baylis and Son Ltd, Worcester

CONTENTS

MEDIA: Print/Vid/Aud

KEYMITS: GB/SPREW 13271482 MITSDISC:

2296 [PN3 PT6 FG5 SM1 PE4 RK9]

US/CALF 36749167 MITSDISC: 2179

[PN78 PT22 FG94]

MITSUFACS: as given

Introduction
THE DINAN COLLECTION

Celia Dinan was born in London almost three centuries ago, in 2007. She died in the west of England at the age of forty. During her lifetime she apparently did nothing to suggest that her name would be remembered by even the most industrious or eccentric researcher into the history of her period. She did not try to make a name for herself in public affairs or in the arts or sciences. Her attachment to the once-notorious Eric Hirn aside, she did not seek the company of those who already were, or were later to become, famous or powerful for any reason. As far as I have been able to find out, her name appeared in contemporary newspapers only twice: on the occasion of her birth, when, in conformity with the practice then current among people of her social class, an advertisement announcing the event appeared in *The Times*; and in the brief reports of her death that were published in several newspapers [PN3:a34]. To judge from these reports just two things made her death worthy of note. The first was that she was a 'peer's daughter'. The second was the failure of a coroner's court to come to a finding as to whether or not she had taken her own life.

Who can tell how long memories of Celia Dinan survived among those who had known her? Lord Dinan died fifteen years after his daughter; the date of Lady Dinan's death is not known; Celia herself was an only child. Once her acquaintances and relations had died, in their turn, it was as if she had never been. Like all but an unimaginably tiny handful of her contemporaries, she was completely forgotten. Since her only child died in infancy, and she did not (so far as we know) donate any of her ovaries to an ovarian bank, nothing even of her physical substance was transmitted to succeeding generations. So she would have remained – not even an absence, if I can put it that way – had it not been for the discovery two years ago of a jumble of papers, among which were the notebooks containing the various chapters or episodes of HER STORY. It was quite by chance that the papers were discovered; by chance too (in a sense) that they were passed on to me for examination. Before going further, therefore, I must say a little about how they were found, the place in which they were found, and the use to which I have put them.

The Abd-el Aziz Islamic Boarding School for Girls stands on the outskirts of Hepney, in the newly created Second Provincial Region West. The main school building is a converted house of stone, built more or less in the shape of a capital E. Most of it dates from the nineteenth century. However, the flat-fronted gables above the main and side entrances, together with the regularity of the small, square bedroom windows in the upper two floors, suggest that parts of it are of an even earlier date. In front of the house there are playing fields protected from prying eyes by tall hedges and even taller fences of flexitex; to the side there is a walled garden; at the back, a new, whitewashed mosque of cataplastic brick, in addition to various other offices and ancillary buildings. The school is in a valley, and the slopes above, which belong to the estate, are well-wooded. In whatever direction you look the horizon is bounded either by summer's green foliage or by the brown and bluish vacancies of autumn and winter. Thus the girls, all of whom are from wealthy homes, and most of whom are destined to become the wives of members of parliament, senior civil servants, army officers, judges, and directors of companies, may be sure of remaining in the seclusion demanded of them by the religion which they and their husbands-to-be follow.

Mardle House, as the Abd-el Aziz school used to be known, has had many owners in the several hundred years of its existence. It was once the home of the scholarly recluse and aristocrat, Roger Shuttaford, author of *Ancient Copper Mines in South Devon*; it has been used as a country hotel and as a boys' boarding school; it served as an officers' mess in one or another of the major twentieth century wars. It has also been a home to a variety of families whose names appear on the title deeds of the property, but about whom little or nothing is known. Some of these purchasers, it would seem, were of local origin; others, like Victor Dinan, settled there after careers that had been made in London or abroad; all of them, given the size of the property, must be assumed to have been well-to-do.

A little over two years ago the present owners, the governors of the school, embarked on a programme of rebuilding and enlargement. One of the jobs undertaken then was the replacement of the roof over the central wing of the building – the middle arm of the E, so to speak. In the course of preliminary investigations of the spaces under the existing roof, the builders discovered that what had always been taken to be a blank wall at the end of the wing was merely a filling-in between two substantial brick buttresses. (These, it is thought, were in all likelihood inserted after the earthquake of 2127.) Inside the cavity thus revealed various inconsequential items were found: ancient electrical ducting; a primitive, metal-plated flashlight, corroded from within; the remains of squares of natural and synthetic materials, blankets in all probability, packed into bags which had themselves long since disintegrated; some large, black, plastic discs used for the recording and transmission of sound. Lying amid this kind of rubbish was a metal trunk with a tight-fitting lid. It was not locked. No labels or lettering of any kind were affixed to the trunk. Since the edges of the lid and those of the trunk itself had rusted together, and the hinges at the back cracked as soon as pressure was put on them, it was opened only after considerable effort. If the builders had hoped that they had come upon a cache of late-twentieth century coins or *objets*, they were to be disappointed. The contents turned out to consist almost entirely of papers. Those on top were yellow and covered with dust; many of them fragmented as soon as they were touched. Most of those beneath were in good condition, however.

The trunk was carried down to the director of the school, Fakhr al Mulik abu Ali. After some consultation with members of his staff, and a transvidi with the chairman of his board of governors, he decided to get in touch with the present writer. Here I should explain that Fakhr al Mulik abu Ali and I have known each other for many years. We are in effect neighbours: my house stands on the corner where the school's private driveway meets the public road. On several occasions we have organised joint functions between his institution and my own (the Hepney College for Mature and Post-Career Students). However, it was primarily in my capacity as founder and

chairwoman for the last twelve years of the Hepney Local
History Association, on behalf of whom I have occasionally
lectured to senior girls in the school, that he turned to me.

All readers or viders of HER STORY will, I hope, realise just how
greatly they are indebted to Fakhr al Mulik abu Ali and the
governors of his school. Had the governors wished to do so,
they would have been perfectly entitled to keep private Celia
Dinan's papers. In fact, when I realised how delicate, from the
religious and theological point of view, the central matter of HER
STORY might be considered to be, the possibility of its being
suppressed did at once occur to me. But so far from putting
obstacles in the way of publication, the governors graciously
authorised me to edit the papers and to present them to the
public in whatever form seemed to me most suitable. Moreover,
the entire collection has since been deposited on permanent
loan in the Hepney Central Library Data Division. Anyone who
wishes to inspect all or any part of it can do so on the KEYMITS
and MITSDISCS given above. MITSUFACS for partial recall are
itemised here wherever this has been deemed appropriate.

The conclusion I came to during my preliminary examination of
the contents of the trunk was that they had been hurriedly
thrown together after Celia Dinan's death. The person who had
collected them – whoever he or she was – had evidently not had
the heart to burn the papers or to dispose of them finally in any
other fashion. So it had been left to others, or to the vicissitudes

of time, to do the job. I can produce no evidence to substantiate this belief; but it is difficult to think of any other explanation for the variety of the material found in the trunk or the confusion in which it was jumbled. A hasty, indiscriminate clearance, a choked tidying-up, a not-quite-getting-rid-of articles which the collector had no use for but which he or she was unable to destroy – this, affectingly enough, after the lapse of about two hundred and fifty years, was what I seemed to confront as I unpacked the trunk item by item. So the old school certificates and school magazines [SM1:u6] had gone in together with the abortive diaries from different periods (SM1:t4]; the stories written in childhood ('Jennifer and the Ghost', 'My Lucky Stars', 'The Talking Teddy') [SM1:t8] with the folders of under-graduate lecture notes [SM1:u12]; address books (SM1:p3] together with photographs crammed anyhow into envelopes and now (alas!) congealed hopelessly and indistinguishably into a single mass; a bound copy of Celia Dinan's Master of Philosophy dissertation presented to London University (enti-tled *The Image of the Madonna in Fifteenth Century Flemish Art*) [SM1:u63] interleaved with private letters [PE4]; used airline tickets and impenetrable-looking documents containing verti-cal and transverse columns of figures which specialists in the period advise me were used for tax-gathering purposes [SM1:g12], along with letters from a bank [SM1:g13] . . . . And of course the notebooks in which she had written, late in her brief life, the various episodes of HER STORY [SM1:t11–19]. Of these notebooks, more will of course be said shortly.

Deciphering the archaic script and orthography of the letters, notebooks, and other handwritten documents, prior to MITSU-BISHING the entire collection, took several months. Further information came to me from a variety of sources, chief among them being the British Library; the National Demographica; the State Commission on Historical Data; the records of the First and Second Guilds (formerly Royal College) of Surgeons; the records of the coroners' offices of the First Provincial Region West and the London Paramountcy; the Victoria and Albert Museum; the Ibn Omar (formerly Courtauld) Institute; the Law Enforcement Co. Inc. of San Bernardino, California (successors to the San Bernardino Police Department); and the Anne-Marie Bickenbeiler Multi-Cult Center of Religious Enquiry at the Westonaria Campus of the University of California. My thanks are due to the chief data officer of each of these institutions, as well as to a number of private collectors and researchers whose names are fully recorded in the Dinan Collection.

Any admirer of HER STORY who goes through the collection must find it ironic that the life of Victor Dinan, Celia's father, should be so much better documented than his daughter's. He was the one whose words were from time to time quoted in the newspapers of the day and whose photograph appeared in them [PN3:v11]; the one on whom various public honours were bestowed – first the honorary degrees and medals, then the 'knighthood', finally the 'life peerage', which transformed Sir

Victor Dinan into the Baron Dinan of Mardle in the County of
Devon. These rewards, together with a great deal of money,
were bestowed on him for his achievements as an orthopaedic
surgeon (he was the inventor of an artificial elbow-joint, known
as the Dinan Hinge, which was considered a great advance in
orthopaedic techniques at the time, but is of course no longer in
use); as an eminent medical administrator (dean of the Royal
College of Surgeons; director of the Joint Council on Medical
School Admissions and Teaching Practices; patron and committee member of the British Association for the Advancement of
Science); and, not least, as a prominent figure in the councils of
the Conservative Party in the west of England.

A healer, an inventor, and an outstanding administrator and
committee man – a formidable array of talents, one might think.
The photographs of Lord Dinan preserved in newspaper files
suggest that he thought so too. Viders who call these up will
note that his head is large, his neck is straight, his eyes are clear,
his features are strong, his grey hair lies flat on either side of a
surgically decisive parting. In some of the photographs [e.g.
PN3:v6] he wears the garments, archaic even then, which were
considered suitable for ceremonial occasions: black robes with
scarlet facings; flat, squashed-looking hats; collars of spotted
fur. According to the obituary eventually published in *The
Times* [PN3:v14] he was 'a surgeon of great skill, integrity, and
ingenuity, with a rare gift for reassuring anxious patients', 'an
admirable teacher', 'a selfless chairman', 'a friend to cherish', 'a
splendid raconteur', and 'a devoted family man who, in later

years, suffered a grievous loss in the death of his adored only child.'

According to that child, on the other hand, he was 'a beast and a bully, who mustn't think that he can do to me what he did to you' [PE4:c16]. The 'you' in question was Celia's mother; the words appear in a letter Celia wrote to her shortly before she left England to live for a while in Australia.

Whom are we to believe? The obituarist of *The Times*? Lord Dinan's daughter? Both of them? Neither? In both cases the evidence we have is of two, perhaps equally unhelpful kinds: the remote, ultimately frigid items which appeared in news-papers; and the all-too heated and intimate scraps of letters and diaries found in the trunk at the Abd-el-Aziz Islamic Boarding School for Girls. What worlds lie between them! And what worlds lie between us and them!

About Celia Dinan's mother we know much less than we do about her father. Indeed, we know little more about her than that she had been, before her marriage, a Miss Yerkes, daughter of a Professor Yerkes of Hull University. No photographs of her seem to have survived; she was not honoured on her death with an obituary notice in *The Times*, or even, it would seem, with a paid announcement. Since we know that she outlived her husband, this last omission suggests that she must also have outlived all her near relations. Like many other Englishwomen of that era, and of the eras that preceded and followed it, her life appears to have been effectively overshadowed or swallowed up by those of her husband and her child.

*   *   *

Celia herself was born in London, and educated at St Paul's
School for Girls and at St John's College, Oxford. (The archives
of neither of these institutions have yielded any useful information about her. Fire, during the Hammersmith Riots of 2135, in
the one case, and flood in the other, have seen to that.)
Subsequently she returned to London and registered as an
'M.Phil.' student at the Courtauld (Ibn Omar) Institute, which
was then one of the large number of institutions affiliated to the
old, unreformed London University. In due course her thesis on
the Madonna in fifteenth century Flemish art was submitted to
the examiners and the degree was awarded to her soon after her
twenty-third birthday.*

During her period in London she apparently shared a flat in
Islington with three or four other students. One of these, Vita
Gill, was to be an important witness at the inquest held after
Celia's death, years later. Letters and postcards show that after
taking her second degree she spent some time in France

---

* In view of what she was to write in HER STORY, the thesis would naturally
appear to be of special interest to us. Viders who call it up, however, might be
disappointed in what they will find. It is a conscientious, docile, youthful piece
of work, littered with the critical jargon of the day and full of deferential
allusions to the work of older critics and scholars. A letter in the file [SM1:u19]
suggests that the choice of thesis-topic was not really Celia's own; it seems
rather that she was judiciously 'steered' towards it by her supervisor. Perhaps
no one would have been more surprised than the author herself, once she had
finished the thesis, if she had been told that the work she had done on it was
never to be put entirely behind her.

[PE4:c18], and some time in Australia [PE4:c20]; it is impossible to say with certitude how long was either of these sojourns. Both were more than mere holidays, however. At the age of twenty-six we find her back in London, established on her own in a flat in Wandsworth and employed by a London publisher as a 'picture researcher'.

Given the background and interests outlined above, her career up to this point appears to have been conventional enough. All that is unconventional about it, perhaps, is that at the time of her departure for Australia she had in effect broken off relations with her father. Or so her letters to her mother strongly suggest. One of them has already been quoted; in another she says explicitly that she 'never want(s) to see him again' [PE4:c14]; in others she refers to him variously as a hypocrite, a liar, a philistine, and a rhinoceros. In those same letters the tone she adopts towards her mother is generally one of pity; sometimes that pity turns into reproach. 'If only you'd put up more of a fight, who knows, I mightn't have had such a struggle with him!' [PE4:c21] – that is a note which is struck several times.

The presence of these letters in the trunk suggests – to this researcher at least – that the person who brought the whole collection together, after Celia's death, was most probably her mother. However that may be, such documents, with all the bitterness they express, make a painful contrast with other items that were to be found lying in promiscuous confusion among them. There is, for instance a birthday card [PE4:d6] with a hand-drawn picture of a little man holding a huge bunch of balloons in his hand; on each of the balloons is a letter; together they spell out *Happy Birthday to a Darling 6-Year Old*; an arrow pointing to the little man's head bears the legend *Your Daddy*. Also to be found in the trunk is a book [RK9:o24] more formally inscribed: *To Celia, who came Top, with love from her Father*. The inscription is dated June 2018 (i.e. when Celia was eleven years old). We do not know in what activity it was that she came 'Top', but the fact that the book is a pocket English-French dictionary may in itself provide us with a clue. There is also a postcard [PE4:d9] from Nairobi, with a picture of several baboons sitting in solemn conclave on some rocks; on the reverse side of the card the sender challenges the recipient to pick him out among them. Apparently Sir Victor (as he was then) had gone to East Africa to attend a medical congress. Just one letter [PE4:d12] from him written to her during her adolescence is to be found; it is affectionate and reassuring ('Don't worry about the money it costs to phone; we love to hear from you') and tells her that he is missing her *quite* as much as she is missing him – 'and probably a bit more!'

How and why father and daughter fell out must remain a mystery to us. It would probably be unwise for us to think of a case about which we know so little as an exemplification of the stresses which, historians tell us, were felt especially acutely within the institution of the family during that remote historical period. Enough for us to stick to the evidence we have, however exiguous some of it may appear to be. What we know for certain about the next stage of Celia Dinan's life is that after almost three years in London she suddenly threw up her job and went to the United States. We know also that she went there because she was induced to do so by the man who had become her lover.

About this man, Eric Hirn by name, the records contain a fair amount of information. Details of his spectacular career are readily available from newspaper and teletape archives in this country and the United States; the best single collection is to be found, not surprisingly, in the data bank of the Anne-Marie Bickenbeiler Multi-Cult Center of Religious Enquiry (US KEYMITS and MITSDISCS given above). The murderous debacle in which Hirn's career ended – the collapse of his colony at Sierra Zafiro, California, his escape, his reappearance in Ecuador, his further and final disappearance – was a great sensation at the time. Then that sensation gave way to others, as it was bound to do, and Eric Hirn and his teachings and his misdeeds were forgotten. Except, of course, by those like Celia, whose lives he had changed or ruined.

The only book Eric Hirn ever wrote has a banal enough title: *The Hidden Voices*. Both the American and British editions [RK:m3/4] are undistinguished looking productions, dressed in blue plasticised covers, with a picture of the author on the back. In the United States this book went into twenty-four editions over a period of three years; in Britain it was reprinted nine times. Those viders who wish to understand its appeal might do best, before reading it, to listen to the tape [PT6:f43] which accompanied the book, and of which the book itself purported to be no more than an explanation or elaboration.

The playing-time of the tape is about an hour. No words are said and no music is played on it; no tune is sung or hummed in the course of it. It consists solely of noises produced, without any artificial aids, over a range of no less than three octaves, by Eric Hirn himself. There are screams, growls, howls, groans, grunts, coos, sobs, whoops, hisses, sighs, snarls, cackles, squeaks, screeches, yelps, bellowings, bayings . . . as well as many other noises for which no words have ever been invented. Some of the noises move up and down the scale; some strike a single, sustained note; some are parts of complex, quasi-musical patterns; almost all, having been uttered once, reappear at different times in unexpected conjunctions or inversions; several of these combinations, and the inflections and intonations employed in producing them, have a tantalising resemblance to language, to recognisable speech. All are gibberish. The tape consists, and is intended to consist, of nothing but gibberish throughout. To produce speech-like gibberish is extremely difficult, as anyone will know who has ever tried to imitate the sounds of a foreign language without being able to speak it; but that is just a minor aspect of the virtuosity of Hirn's performance. The tape is in truth a frightening, even an uncanny item to listen to. In its way it is far more impressive than the book which accompanies it.

It is also more impressive than the appearance of the man responsible for it. The face that looks out from the back cover of the book is a commonplace and inexpressive one. Plump, cleanshaven, balding, not youthful, bespectacled, Eric Hirn reveals to his readers a bulging brow, capacious nostrils, and a rather primly pursed mouth. He looks like a determined clerk. From that nose and closed mouth one might expect to hear little but a persistent, even remorseless, stertorousness. There is no allure in the eyes; at any rate none that one can discern over the gulf of the centuries. The spectacles he wears sit rather low on his nose, and are of a rimless, 'half-moon' pattern quite fashionable at that time. Did he, one cannot help wondering irreverently, take them off before beginning his vocal exercises?

Then one turns to the book itself. Its argument can be summarised as follows. Our souls and bodies are one. The essential oneness of our beings is most strikingly manifest to us in our gift of speech. In its actions and effects the voice is at once physical and spiritual; muscular and mental; private and public; human and divine. It is through our voices that we are bound together in societies; by virtue of our voices that we have been endowed with the power of reflexive and transcendental thought. It follows then, according to Eric Hirn, that when we speak or sing with a constricted voice we reveal the constrictions not only of our bodies but also of our souls, of our spiritual capacities. All such constrictions arise ultimately from our fear of what is in ourselves; and that which we fear above all, which we attempt to suppress or flee from is the God within us: the very God who comes into being in and through our speech. It is there, at the intersection of body and soul, individual and society, individual and self (in reflexivity) – at that intersection that God exists. He exists, however, only to the extent to which we are able to express or evoke him in our voices.

As a result of the false upbringing of which we have all been the victims, the argument continues, our usual impulse is to contain him, or deny him, to try to escape from him. But we have the power to liberate him, too, if we would dare to do so; if we would learn to wail and laugh again as we had done when we were children, grunt and roar as we had done when we were animals, hiss as we had done when we were reptiles, chirp as we had done when we were birds, sigh as we had done when we were grass and trees, groan as we had done when we were rocks. Only then would the spirit and matter of which we are constituted be reunited; only then could the individual be rejoined to the infinite and once again learn to accommodate it within him; only thus would we come to know ourselves as literally the inspiration and exhalation of God – both his creator and conduit, the place of his coming into being.

For a fee, Eric Hirn would undertake to enable you to utter through yourself what he called alternately and interchangeably 'the Voice of God' and 'the God of Voice'. The initial fee you paid, in effect, by buying his book and the accompanying tape; subsequently, if you entrusted yourself to his care, a kind of physico-spiritual therapy would 'deconstrict' your voice and thus liberate the deity hidden within you. At one time, during the period of Eric Hirn's greatest efflorescence, the full course of 'deconstriction' therapy was offered only to those who took up residence in the colony of Sierra Zafiro, in Southern California, which had room for no less than three hundred and fifty would-be 'deconstrictionists' at a time. These pupils, or patients, were attended by a staff of some thirty Hirn-trained assistants, as well as by a number of housekeepers, gardeners, and security men. Eventually the stories that runaway deconstrictionists told first to the press and then to the police were to lead to a raid on Sierra Zafiro by officers from the San Bernardino County police force. After a brief but bloody gunbattle with some of Hirn's assistants the police managed to take possession of the place: grounds, gardens, stores, residences for staff and pupils, punishment block for dissidents, 'pharmacy' (the administration of mood-changing drugs had become an important part of Hirn's practice), and of course the master's private apartments and private safe.

But of the man himself there was no trace. Apparently he had had informants within the local police department and had slipped away unnoticed a little time before the raid. He had clearly not wanted to precipitate a stampede among his followers which might hinder his own getaway. His subsequent adventures in Ecuador are not really our business. All that needs to be said here is that he managed to escape from police custody in Quito, while he was being held during extradition proceedings; and that thereafter nothing was ever heard of him.

Nothing at all. Possibly he settled down under an assumed name in Ecuador itself or in some other part of the world; it may be that some of those who had helped him to enter the country, and to escape from its police, had their own reasons for getting rid of him. Eventually, several years later, long after Celia Dinan's death, a group of his former disciples was to gather in a farmhouse in Wales, with the intention of perpetuating his teachings; they claimed to be regularly in touch with him by means of an extra-terrestrial communications system (KOSMO-VOX) available only to him and themselves.

How Hirn first met Celia Dinan – whether through the publishing firm for which she worked, or in some other context – is not known. The proof copy [RK9:m2] of his book which was found among her papers contains a number of marginal notes in her hand, as well as many running corrections, most of which consist of her Anglicisation of his American spellings. One might assume this was done in preparation for the first English edition of the book, which appeared in the autumn of 2036. By the time that edition appeared, however, Celia was living with its author in New York. Her departure with him seems to have been arranged in great haste. Perhaps he had reasons for clearing out of Britain which he could not divulge to her. So hurried was their departure that Lady Dinan learned her daughter had given up her flat, job, and residence in London only when she received a letter from Celia, from New York,

[PE4:c64], in which she was asked to pick up various items in the flat, to get rid of everything else, and to instruct a firm of agents to sell the balance of the lease.

We know nothing about Celia's relationships with men before the arrival of Eric Hirn. From the depth of her infatuation with him one might be tempted to believe that he was her first lover – unlikely though that must seem, given what we understand to have been the *mores* of the time, and given also her age when she met him. She writes to her mother as if nothing now had any reality for her but the prospect of sharing her life with Hirn, of working with him, of learning from him. Her letters from New York [PE4:c66] speak of their life together with what can only be described as a cosy or intimate sense of wonder. His name appears on almost every other line: what he wants, what he does, what he shows her, what he sees, says, believes, hopes, even what he eats and drinks. There are, incidentally, more letters to her mother in the file from this period – during her stay in New York and the first few months of their subsequent, perhaps inevitable, transfer to California – than from any other period of her life.

The first hint that the idyllic phase of their relationship was coming to its end is to be found in a letter [PE4:c71] written fairly soon after their arrival in California. In it Celia writes that she and Eric have moved into a house belonging to someone by the name of Denise, who, with her husband, was also a disciple of Eric's. (She uses the word 'disciple' without putting it into quotation marks, it should be noted: that is to say, without embarrassment or irony.) They were going to try to set up a therapeutic centre, she writes, for the study and dissemination of Eric's teachings, and for the training of a further generation of therapists. However, towards the end of this letter she makes an admission: 'It's going to be difficult, after having had Eric all to myself over these past months, to share him with others.'

A month later there is a suggestion in another letter [PE4:c76] that the 'sharing' she had to get used to was of a more thoroughgoing kind than anything she had probably bargained for. Though her language is guarded – she could hardly be expected to speak directly to her mother of such matters, even in those times – it appears that Denise, who had been Eric's lover in the past, had taken up this position once again ('I did not know how close they'd been with one another – and still are!'). This did not mean, however, that Hirn was proposing to dispense with any of Celia's services. 'I find things very difficult to cope with,' she says, before adding conscientiously, 'even though I understand that a man like Eric could hardly be satisfied for long with whatever I alone am able to give him – and am still *glad* to give him. The demands he makes of everyone around him, the demands he makes of himself, can't be measured by the standards that apply to ordinary people, and I must resign myself to this. Or rather, accept it gratefully.'

Presumably she tried to do just that for as long as Hirn wished or allowed her to. In the little household described in her letters we can in fact discern the rudiments of the Sierra Zafiro colony and of the scandals within it that were later to

keep the press and television screens on both sides of the
Atlantic busy for a few weeks. The very notion of a centre
dedicated to the spreading of Hirn's doctrines, and run by him
with the aid of a group of devotees, is a foreshadowing of
greater things to come. The references (e.g. PE4:c73) which
Celia makes to the money that had been kept for her in a family
trust, and which she now intended to give to her lover, provide
early evidence of how he was going to manage the finances of
Sierra Zafiro. His insistence on having more than one companion at a time to share his bed was to be proclaimed (and
obeyed) on a positively grandiose scale in that institution.

Hirn was installed there, in Sierra Zafiro, within two years of
his arrival in California. That was how fast his movement had
grown. By then there was already a waiting-list of candidates
for admission to the place; a hastily trained corps of therapists
were at work within it; a press and recording studio were
putting out edition after edition of his masterpiece; there were
even plans afoot to establish satellite versions of Sierra Zafiro in
the state of Florida, in Great Britain, and in Australia. After
twenty years of endeavour – initially as a would-be opera
singer, the rest in the healing or shamanistic line – Hirn was at
last enjoying, on a huge scale, the fruits of success.

As for Celia, who moved into Sierra Zafiro with the pioneers
of the settlement, and who gave birth to a baby boy within a
month or two of the move, she had by then clearly ceased to be
of importance to him. She was not a member of the 'monitorium' which, under their leader's guidance, actually ran the

place; she had not been admitted to the ranks of the therapists, who were next in the hierarchy; she was nothing more, indeed, than a subordinate worker in the nursery in which all the community's infants lived. This at least enabled her, as she wrote to her mother in one of the scant letters from this period [PE4:c85], to spend more time with her baby than she might otherwise have been able to do. In these letters she refers occasionally to Hirn (how could she not?), but they never speak of him as the father of the child; as a matter of fact, the father is identified by name in none of them. So we cannot ultimately be sure who he was. Even the baby's name is of no help here. At the command of the monitorium, all children born in Sierra Zafiro were given the surname Sapphire – this by way of tribute to the place of their birth and to the mystical bonds supposedly uniting all those who resided there. Celia was at least permitted to choose her baby's first name. She called him Basil. He was not to have long to enjoy either appellation.

Only in their references to her baby or to others among her tiny charges do her letters from Sierra Zafiro show any vitality or pleasure. What she made of everything else around her, of what Hirn was doing, of her own position, of the bizarre mixture of conventicle, holiday camp, hospital, criminal band, and detention-centre which Hirn's great experiment had become, we simply do not know. Even if she had wished to write to her mother in any but approving fashion she would have had difficulty in doing so, as all letters from Sierra Zafiro were censored by the monitorium. Nor would she have been able to leave without the monitorium's permission: whether or not she applied for such permission is not known. Since all newspapers and radios and television sets capable of receiving programmes from the outside world were forbidden in Hirn's domain, it is also impossible for us to guess how aware she might have been, towards the end, of the storm that was about to break over the place.

As ill-luck would have it, the nursery suffered particularly badly during the police assault on the settlement. Of the four people killed in the attack, two were children. Little Basil Sapphire, who died of inhaling smoke and tear-gas, was one of these. His first birthday had been celebrated just a few weeks before.

The newscasts put out soon after the attack, and preserved most fully for us in the archives of the Bickenbeiler Center [PT22:f61], show the charrings and fragmentings of diminutive beds and tables in the nursery; they show broken toys, scarred walls, a tiled floor stained with blood. They also show, in the background, a handful of distraught women gazing at the scene, or turning away, or running from it. Any vider who calls up this material is bound to wonder, perhaps with a certain guilty curiosity, if he is looking unawares at Celia in the hour of her bereavement. Could she be that one staring forward? That one whose whole body is skewed or clamped in shock? That one gesticulating? That one trying to comfort another? The one being comforted? Or any of those hiding their faces as they are put in line to be interviewed by the police? Pale or dark blobs that they are, we can enlarge them, shrink them, turn them back, speed them up, slow them down, animate them again by ancient grief, stun them again by ancient trauma. Yet they retain the dignity of being forever beyond our grasp. Certainly Celia is not to be found among the women who actually speak to the camera, all of whose names are given and all of whom have American accents. Even in the midst of the carnage some talk of their relief at the end of what they call 'a nightmare'; others denounce the 'martyrdom' of Eric Hirn and the destruction of 'a healing, saving community'.

It is a remarkable fact that none of the papers in the trunk which are dated after the death of Celia's child ever refer to him. This abstention or absence has its own eloquence, of course. Moreover, none of the papers, with one exception, make any direct or indirect allusion to the end of Sierra Zafiro. The exception is a certificate issued by the San Bernardino Police Department, dated a fortnight after the attack (SM1:g7], which states formally that the department has no objection to Ms Celia Dinan leaving the country; this on the strength of an undertaking given by her to obey the terms of any subpoena which might subsequently be served on her, in any part of the world. Since the report of the judicial commission of inquiry which was appointed to investigate events at Sierra Zafiro [FG94] refers several times to the death of Basil Sapphire (infant), but presents no evidence in the matter taken from his mother, we must conclude either that no subpoena demanding her appearance before the commission was issued, or that (safe from prosecution in Great Britain) she simply broke the terms of the undertaking she had given.

Paradoxically, perhaps, the documentation available to us becomes more fragmentary as a result of Celia's return to London, and her biography in some ways more difficult to follow. Instead of the letters she had been writing to her mother, not to speak of the evidence provided by newspapers and newscasts, we have to make do with a few diary-like but random scribblings which went into a floral-covered little notebook, and were apparently intended for the eye of the writer only [SM1:t9]; the story also has to be eked out with scraps of hospital records and studiously uncommunicative communications from doctors [SM1:p18]; with letters begun and abandoned [PE4:c95]; with a diary of appointments [SM1:p27]; with summaries of evidence eventually given by people in the coroner's court [FG5:n14].

Putting all these sources together, and allowing for errors in the conclusions that may be drawn from them, we know that Celia returned directly to England from California. For the first time she visited Mardle House, the home her parents had bought for themselves in what was then the county of Devon, and which was eventually to be the place where her *nachlass* came to rest. Under the stress of events a reconciliation had apparently taken place between herself and her father; one can only hope that both of them found consolation in it. After a spell in the country – how long it was we do not know – she went back to London, where she tried, gallantly enough, to re-establish herself: to make a 'new life' for herself, as we like to say in such circumstances.

She managed to get a job in the Victoria and Albert Museum in South Kensington: rather a lowly job, which involved her in sitting behind a counter for much of the day and selling books and picture postcards. Later she found employment in an architectural bookshop in Bloomsbury Square, where she seems to have found the work more congenial. However, her misfortunes were not yet at an end. After about a year in London she was admitted to hospital for a series of tests. As a result of these a growth was discovered in the lining of the uterus. An operation followed. In those days surgery was the only treatment available for the condition from which she was suffering. On her discharge from the hospital she knew that she would never be able to have another child. But the doctors were at least able to assure her that the growth had not been malignant and that there was no reason for her to be anxious about her health in the future.

So she went back to work. About the next three years of her life we know little. It might even be said that the only source of information we have about her state of mind during this time is the text of HER STORY itself, which she seems to have begun towards the end of the period. Naturally I am aware, in making this suggestion, that it would be a gross error to look for direct parallels between her own experiences and the events described in her fable. The very point of the fable is surely the otherness of the world it enabled her to inhabit while she was writing it. Her life is what she wrote *out of*, not what she wrote *about*: a difficult but essential distinction for us to keep in mind if we are to do justice both to the author and her tale. At the same time anyone who goes through HER STORY is bound to feel that it reveals to us, in its highly refracted, imaginative fashion, more of the writer's passions of grief and anger, of longing and bewilderment, of remorse and incredulity, than any direct outburst could. Of her loneliness too. Only in and through this work of fiction, set in a period so remote from her own, about a woman so unlike herself, could she continue the struggle to find out what she believed; only through it, more painfully still, could she compel herself to believe what she had found out.

For the rest, there is almost nothing in the papers to tell us how she lived, what new friendships, if any, she managed to establish, or on what footing she had put her relationship with her parents. Inevitably, readers and viders of HER STORY will be tempted to ask a number of questions which the story itself will have provoked or prompted. Did she, during this time, become a haunter of churches? An offerer of prayers? A watcher of others offering theirs? An attender of Bible classes? Someone who lingered in parks near mothers and their infants? A student once again of Renaissance art and sculpture? A reader of her own thesis on the figure of the Madonna in Flemish art?

Are we to imagine her going to work in Bloomsbury Square, returning alone to her flat in Marchmont Street nearby, preparing her dinner, watching television, listening to the radio, reading, beginning to write HER STORY on scraps of paper which have been lost to us? Or is this image of solitude and reserve simply too tempting, too obvious, to be truthful? Did she have any special male friends at this time, and if so who were they? What, if anything, did she tell her acquaintances of the life she had led in California, and did any of Hirn's associates attempt to communicate with her?

Unanswerable questions, all of them. No letters survive from this passage of her life; she did not indulge herself, as she had occasionally in the past, in intermittent diary-like scribblings. Instead she turned in another direction. The exact date of her beginning the writing of HER STORY cannot be finally determined. But there are some strong clues indicating the period which she devoted to it. In spring of the year 2045 she took a cruise to several countries in the Middle East, including Egypt and Israel (as most of the area now falling into the Arabian Republic of Al-Quds was at that time called): a suggestive journey for her to have made, in the circumstances. We know about this trip because of the presence in the trunk of a plastic pouch bearing the name of a firm of travel agents stamped in gilt lettering on it. In this pouch was found an itinerary [SM1:g14] for a trip made by Ms Celia Dinan and Ms Vita Gill.

This piece of evidence is merely circumstantial, I admit: it certainly does not provide us with the earliest possible date (*terminus a quo*, as the scholars say) at which she could have commenced the task. She could well have decided, for instance, to go to the Near East because her curiosity about it had been aroused by what she had already written, rather than the other way around. However, in a batch of unused pages at the back of the second of the notebooks in which she was writing the tale there appears the draft of a letter dated 12 September 2045 [SM1:t12]. The letter itself has nothing to do with HER STORY: it is addressed to a firm of plumbers who have done some work in the bathroom of her flat: she was writing to tell them that what they had done was so unsatisfactory she had decided to withhold payment of their bill. This trivial, domestic piece of evidence seems to me little short of decisive. The notebook must have been lying on her desk for her to have used it for that purpose; it could only have been there because she was preoccupied with the writing that fills most of the other pages in it.

Of course, just as we do not know how long before that date she had begun the tale, so we cannot say how much longer she continued with it. Nor do we know in what sequence the various notebooks were filled or abandoned. None then was numbered by the author; the numbers given to them here are my own, and simply follow a 'chronological' ordering of the story they tell. That is, they begin with a birth and end with a death.

Her own end was not that far off. In the summer of 2046 she was admitted to hospital for a further series of tests. Another operation was performed and she was discharged after a few days, again with assurances from the doctors about how things should go with her in the future. At this point the evidence does not merely remain thin, as before, but becomes positively obscure as well; wilfully obscure, if one may so put it. From the evidence of the notebook mentioned earlier [SM1:t9] and from letters produced at the inquest (see below), it seems that Celia herself did not accept at face value the assurances she had been given. From then on she apparently began to believe that she was seriously ill; that she was suffering from cancer; and that the doctors were deliberately withholding the truth of her condition from her. ('They're trying to protect me,' she writes bleakly at one point. 'Why? What is there to protect?') It may be that the conviction which took hold of her, or of which she seemed with a certain eagerness to take hold, sprang from a generalised depressive or melancholic state of mind; it may be that she was suffering from a physical ailment which the rudimentary medical procedures of the day were incapable of diagnosing; there is also the possibility that her suspicions about the doctors' assurances had a grounding in fact. Nothing among her papers, anyway, suggests that there was any change of mood or mind on her part over the months that followed.

On 17 March 2047 Celia left London, accompanied by her friend Vita Gill, to drive in her own car to her parents' house in the west country. The travellers did not take the direct route, but chose to do some touring on the way. On the late afternoon of 21 March they arrived in the town of Bideford in North

Devon (now First PRW), and booked in for the night at a hotel. The car was parked on the quayside, to the north of the town-centre. The two women inspected the modest attractions the town had to offer: they crossed and re-crossed the old bridge over the Torridge, and walked in the park beyond the quay, with its guardian-statue of a local author, Charles Kingsley. Then they had dinner in the hotel. Over dinner they shared, according to Miss Gill's account, a single bottle of wine. After dinner Celia left her companion and returned to the quayside, ostensibly to pick up an item from a suitcase that she had left in the car. Some minutes later a passer-by saw the car, with Celia at the wheel, drive straight over the edge of the quay into the river. (The rails standing there today were not in place then.) The tide was in and the river was at its height. The stranger raised the alarm immediately, but by the time the men from the local fire brigade arrived – their station was just a few hundred yards away – it was too late to save her. The car was not dredged from the river until the following day. All the doors, the driver's included, were locked from within. On the previous evening the firemen had had to smash the window on that side in order to get to the body.

The records of the coroner's court show that none of the facts so far given were regarded as contentious [FG5:n14]. For the rest Vita Gill's evidence remained unequivocal. Celia had been relaxed and cheerful throughout dinner and before it; she had left the hotel in a completely casual manner to go to the car, with an assurance that she would be back in a few minutes. She must, the witness insisted, have been attempting to re-park the car on the quay, for some reason, or to bring it closer to the hotel, when an inexplicable and catastrophic error had led to the accident.

However, evidence was also brought forward to show that no fault had been found with the car's brakes, steering, or accelerator; the passer-by who had raised the alarm told the court that the vehicle had seemed to accelerate, if anything, as it had approached the edge of the quay. He agreed that this may have been the consequence of panic rather than intention. Two letters to the court were also admitted as evidence: one from a hospital doctor and the other from Celia Dinan's general practitioner. The first letter stated that the deceased had failed, obviously of set purpose, to keep the last two of the 'follow-up' appointments which had been thought necessary after her discharge from the hospital. The second letter reported that she had appeared to be 'in a kind of traumatised calm' when the writer had last seen her; her psychological condition had definitely given him cause for unease, but she had dismissed out of hand his suggestion that she might be in need of help in this regard.

Suicide? Accident? The consequences of drinking perhaps much more than the single bottle of wine which the faithful and defensive Vita Gill admitted to? Not just any one of these, but rather all of them at once, as it were: the kind of accident that might well befall anyone in a state of despair or distraction? I suspect that not even the ghost of Celia herself, could we only summon it to our aid, would be able to choose decisively among these possibilities.

Once the inquest was over, the body was taken back to London for a private cremation.

Celia Dinan wrote HER STORY in eleven, identical, hard-covered, orange-coloured, wire-bound notebooks. These, as I have said, are not numbered. Viders who call them up will see that each has the words HER STORY in block capitals, in thick, inked strokes, on its cover. Printed on the cover there appears also the legend 'W.H. Smith Notebook': the name 'W.H. Smith' being that of an extensive chain of newspaper and stationery shops which used to operate in many parts of Great Britain. On some of the covers the author has drawn lines in such a way as to make the words HER STORY appear to hang in a frame from the printed title; on others it is the printed matter that she has framed and left hanging from her own lettering. On one [SM1:t16] her title is written transversely to the trade-name – the 'O' of Notebook serving also as the 'O' of STORY – so that together they make up the shape of a cross. Given her subject-matter, this must surely be a deliberate visual pun.

In every case only one side of the ruled pages in the book has been used. Since the books open vertically, as it were, this makes it easy for the reader to flip quite rapidly through them. It is clear that some kind of nervous tic or superstition compel-

led the author to start every new episode in a new notebook; as
a result empty pages remain in all of them; in some cases
practically every page in a book has been left empty. Occasional
random scribblings – shopping lists, names of books, inexplicable numbers – appear in what are otherwise unused pages.
There are also a few drawings or doodles here and there; none
appears to be of any relevance of what she was writing below or
above. The author was evidently fond of drawing chevron
patterns of great complexity during moments of idleness or
frustration.

Readers and viders will hardly need to be reminded that in
Celia Dinan's day most people in Britain, in Western Europe,
and the Americas gave their allegiance, nominally at least, to
the Christian religion. Indeed, the Anglican version of Christ-
ianity was then the offical or 'established' religion in Great
Britain. In writing HER STORY she was therefore able to take for
granted a knowledge of the Gospels which may not be so
readily available in this country today – now that the Anglican
church has for so long been disestablished, and Islam has
become the religion most widely followed by those in Britain
who profess a recognised faith of any kind. However, this
presentation has not been burdened with systematic references
to the passages in the Gospels to which the author makes
allusion or which she appears to bend to her own narrative
purposes. The main features of the story told there are surely
still sufficiently well-known to render that unnecessary. Those

who wish to have the references, however, will find them available on call, together with an account of the historical period which has been LINGUALEX checked for dispassion [RK9:r2].

The file offers no clues as to whether she ever showed what she had written to any of her friends, or considered offering for publication either this version of HER STORY or any projected revision of it.

When I first began turning over the papers which had come to me in such an unexpected and haphazard fashion, I could not help feeling like something of an intruder. It was as if time had interposed a kind of one-way mirror between myself and Celia Dinan, which enabled me to look at her but forbade her from looking at me. After I had started reading HER STORY, however, this feeling left me and was replaced by something like its opposite. In effect, I suddenly seemed to find myself under the author's scrutiny. Perhaps others will have a similar experience. They may also come to feel, as I eventually did, that the period Celia lived in, and the even more distant period she wrote about, are not as different from our own as we sometimes wish to believe.

HER STORY is no more than a fantasy, a reverie, a piece of guesswork, an angular or unexpected filling-in of the most familiar of sacred tales; it is at once a source of consolation for the author and a fierce repudiation of the wish to be consoled.

Being wholly a fiction it reveals to us, as nothing else could, the sense she had of her own being – and of ours.

Naoko Kamikatazawa
Chairwoman, Hepney Local History Association
July 2296

HER STORY

First
WH SMITH NOTEBOOK

Paintings in frames, marble gestures of hope and sorrow, wooden or waxen dolls with gilt crowns on their heads and lilies at their bare feet, mosaics flickering like fish in the light and shadow of a hundred candles ... Depictions of her are everywhere. Beseechings without number go up to her daily. Her stories are known to everyone.

But you? Nobody has ever heard of you. You have no name. It is too late to give you one now. If I imagine you to be a distant kinswoman of hers, perhaps, or merely someone who lived in a village not all that far from her own; a woman whose life may have resembled hers in this respect or that, but differed greatly from it in many others – who can correct me? Not you! You least of all! For years you were hardly so much as an idea in my mind; even less than a possibility, a fleeting speculation, a faint figure that vanished every time I looked for it. Now I feel that you have taken to looking for me. You haunt me. You wait until I am on my own; then I see you gesturing towards me, mutely appealing to me to put words in your mouth, thoughts in your mind, feelings in your heart, sensations in your body, a child in your womb. To give you a chance!

Very well then. I shall try. Women like you are always to be found: unknown, anonymous, taken-for-granted women. There is never a shortage of them. No shortage of children for them either. No end of hope, and of the loss of hope. All I have to do is let one word suggest the next and the truth about you is bound to emerge; the only truth I am capable of depicting at any rate. One without miracles, wonders, prefigured compensations for ineluctable pains. You were not picked out for those. What you went through, you went through on your own, in all the vulnerability of an unredeemed ignorance. Hence your appeal.

It is very different from hers. Only she could be who she is – forever. But you? Anyone could have been you. Even me.

Second
WH SMITH NOTEBOOK

Coming out of you he was huge, an irresistible force you were much too weak to contain or control. It compelled you to do its work. It split you like a husk in order to finish off what it (not you) had begun. Swaddled, upturned, creased, exhausted, feeling for the first time the possibility of its own pain, this mighty force shrank to a frail morsel, a tender thing of skin and whorls, a germ which could do no more than twitch and flutter parts of itself. Or it slept, drawing breaths too soft to be heard, too small to be seen. Or it gazed upward, out of an immense calm, with steady, unseeing, indigo eyes.

That was what amazed you most about the birth: not the pain you went through, but the contrast between the size of the baby as he made his way out of you and the size of him when you held him in your arms for the first time.

You held him. You nursed him. This took place not in a stable, among the incurious beasts, but on a simple bed of wood and leather, in the hut that you had only recently begun to think of as 'home'. It stood alongside others, against the wide hillside. A stream loitered down from the brow of the hill, turning and twisting in wayward fashion among a litter of boulders. Small, tilled fields and orchards had been cleared in places; sheep and goats, guarded by boys, grazed where they could. You had heard their bleating and coughing during the birth and after it, and had not been able to tell the noises they had made from your own.

No shepherds or kings came with gifts to your bedside; none of the animals knelt before you. Instead your mother and the women from the neighbouring houses took care of you. They told you how well you had done; they said what a fine boy he was; they assured you he was like every other healthy baby. Holding him, you were filled with wonder not only at his tininess and frailty, after all he had put you through, but also with incredulity at how short a time had passed since you were a child and had been held by others as you were holding him now. It made you breathless to think of it. Your secret misgiving was that if your baby knew what a baby *you* were, he would cry more loudly than ever; he would feel that you had betrayed him. Poor thing! To be the child of a child; the child of someone whose own childhood had ended (if it had ended) the day before the beginning of his . . .

All young mothers must have such feelings; how could they not? But to you they seemed quite new, singular to yourself, too childish (precisely!) to be spoken of to others.

The sun rose and set; you drank the gruel that was said to be good for you; you woke to the baby's cry and guided his head to your breast, your nipple to his lips. You did not know if the protective passion you felt for him depleted you further, or was a source of refreshment. Or could it possibly have been both at the same time? You slept when you could. Then your lying-in was over and you limped outdoors. The light outside was not so much bright as large; it seemed even larger, somehow, than the spaces it revealed. The sun, on its way down, was about to sink into a band of cloud, like flame-reddened smoke. Every notch in the crest of the hill immediately above the village could be seen against the sky. More distant hills, facing the west, still exposed to the sun, were paler in colour and smoother in outline. Smells of sheep dung and warm stone scented the air. This was the afternoon of your recovery, of your return to the world, and everything your eye fell on, every blade of grass and pebble, seemed to be wrapped or locked silently within itself, charged with a special significance, tense with expectancy. Then you realised that the special significance these objects had was in fact that of belonging to an afternoon like every other. They knew nothing of what had happened to you or to your child; they never would. Hence the power they had over you.

It was a relief to get back into the darkness of the hut and to feel the negligible weight of the baby on your lap once again. He lay there as if on a platform, and, bowed over him, engrossed in what you had made, you pondered and puzzled over why it should have been his completeness, the very absence of anything unfinished about him, that made him seem so vulnerable to you. It was as if his transparent fingernails actually exposed him to the dangers of the world; the just-discernible line of his eyebrow too; even his earnest sneezes . . .

On the eighth day a group of men came and the baby was circumcised. One sat on a stool and held him, one leaned over him and said the prayers, one carried him on a pillow. They were all people from the village, men you knew; there was nothing special about them. Yet on this occasion they bore themselves with an air of much self-importance. You remained outside the room. You heard the murmur of adult, masculine voices, broken by the sudden cry of the child. There. It had been done. Pain had been inflicted on him. Blood had been drawn.

Then the men who had done it hastily handed him back to you, so that you could comfort him with milk, while they comforted themselves with wine. They were less solemn now; they smiled at what they had done, as if they were proud of it, yet relieved also to have it over. For the baby, though, it was not over; nor for you. He was not to be soothed. He would not take the breast. He lay away from you and seemed not so much to draw his breath as to hunt for it, with long, self-stifling shudders between each cry. Eventually he fell asleep. For the next few days his cry had a different note from the one that had already become familiar to you. The sound was sharper now. He was stung into his cry, each time.

It did not take long for the wound to heal. Then the incision that had been made in him, the shape that had been given to the part of him, became in your eyes just another among the beauties he was composed of. Or from which he composed himself, moment by moment. For it was not just this or that feature or movement which you adored every time it caught your attention – curve of cheek it might be, moist lip, white of eye, solemn little heel dangling free – it was rather that each of these belonged to all the others, and they to it, in a never-ending fluctuation, which was nothing less than the whole person, the unique infant.

He was a good baby. Firm, alert, a strong feeder, a deep sleeper, a quiet contemplator of – what? Who knows? Who can remember? How different our lives might be if we *could* remember what it was like to gaze at the world through such unsullied, unalarmed eyes; to be so trusting of our own weakness and so attentive in our own passivity; to be able to hurl ourselves with such frenzy into our cries. When his bouts of crying were brief, you positively enjoyed them, they were so

shameless. When they went on for a long time the noise turned
into a kind of clawing or tearing at a membrane within your
skull, or even deeper than that, right inside your spine, which
you had not previously known to be there. No one else had ever
tampered with it. It made you feel you were being driven crazy
by the baby's undifferentiated grief or anger and your incom-
petence to deal with him. Driven crazy by your husband's
anxiety, too.

At last I mention him! It has taken so long that anyone might
be forgiven for thinking you did not have one. But you did,
indeed you did; and here he is, gesturing to you at every cry or
whimper from the baby, turning to you with a perpetual air of
inquiry, demanding of you that you be expert in all subjects to
do with the child. He turns to you as if anxiety and ignorance
could never visit you; as if you are not also being compelled to
contend with new passions, for which your previous experience has prepared you not at all. Poor man! Every time he looks
at the baby he reveals his fear of the little creature; or rather, his
fear of what it might cost him to feel for it. You are luckier: it
has been so easy for you to love the baby; all you have had to do
is to provide him with what he needs and you have found
yourself loving him; loving and providing have been one,
indistinguishable from each other. For your husband, though,
everything turns into a problem, a puzzle, a source of uncer-
tainty. Even his neighbours are a problem to him; so how could
his child, who is so small, so simple, so unfathomable, not be
another? Speech is a problem to him; silence likewise; so is the

gaze he fixes on you, which is steady and sombre, and yet shakes always with the faintest tremor. Not once, not in the first few months of the marriage, not now, have you ever been drawn to feed on him, graze or brood over him, as if through your eyes and hands you could draw in a sustenance you had never tasted before. He has always known it, but only now do you know it too. Now that that sustenance has been given to you, it seems inconceivable you could have lived without craving for it.

No, it is not towards him that you are drawn. Touchings, lookings, smellings, fondlings, caressings, huggings, holdings, dreamings, sighings, you keep for the baby alone; or he in your arms, under your gaze, irresistibly evokes them. When he feeds from you, you feed from him.

Long before a baby takes a step, you remember how his bowed, loose legs incline towards one another at the heels? His did. Long before a baby speaks, you remember how he has a speech of no words, of pure sound, a kind of song, as tentative and yet as self-assured as a bird's? He spoke to you in that language. You remember how a crying baby will put his head back and reveal harmless gums, wet tongue, parallel ridges on the roof of his mouth, and all the rage within? He cried like that. You know how a baby boy will unknowingly rehearse the careers he may one day follow and the persons he may one day become: fat merchant, street urchin, tramp, soldier, senator, flirt, madman, fever victim? These, lying on his back, or crawling, or rising and standing on infirm ankles, or pursuing with hunched shoulders his own runaway legs, or sitting propped up against a wall, or looking up unexpectedly, or dropping off to sleep on a supporting lap – all these, and many others, were the roles he rehearsed. You know how fleeting are all such foreshadowings of what may never be? Just so fleeting were his. You remember how much mourning there is in motherhood, even in joyful motherhood, even when the child prospers; how constant is your sense of change in what you love and thus of a snatching from you of that which you love – this impossible thing, this embodiment of transience, this child? Well, all that, too, he made known to you. Nor would you have thought it possible, before he came, bringing and taking away so much, that mourning could be so bright, loss so rich, gain so poignant, the tiniest, most casual flickers of limb or eyelash capable of scoring such deep grooves in the heart.

Then you fell pregnant again. Again you had to carry the burden that would, when its time came, split and rend you. Again it did so. It was easier this time, yet also no less cataclysmic. While it was happening there was nothing but *it* in the world. Then it was over, and another infant boy was put in your arms. One of the women went outside to bring in the older boy, who had been banished to a neighbouring hut. Barefoot, soft-kneed, dressed in a tiny tunic that barely covered his loins, his hand in the woman's, his head on a level with yours, where you lay on the low cot, he came in and halted just past the threshold, intimidated by the strangeness of what was afoot. You called him and held out the baby to him. But he was not to

be enticed; stiff, suddenly superfluous, even to himself, he was
incapable of meeting your gaze. Seeing him so disconsolate, at
once so infantile and so adult, you burst into tears. Whereupon,
without having seen him move, you found yourself holding
him and the new baby in a single, fierce embrace. In the heat of
the birth-bed only his skin, from outside it, felt cool.

Now it seemed to you that you really had become the mother
of a family and were no longer a child or girl masquerading as
one. When you walked in the village you had a child in your
arms and another holding on to your hand, taking solemn steps
to keep up with you. When one of them was ill or restless at
night, you feared not only for him but for the other as well.
Sometimes you even muddled their names. You mildly com-
pared them with one another, in looks, in the progress they
made, in temperament, and found pleasure in discerning the
resemblances and differences between them; you also com-
pared, and shrank from comparing, the love you felt for each.
Your husband's presence no longer weighed on you as it had
previously; though he himself was no easier than he had been,
he was merely one of four now. But he was your husband still.
Soon, sooner than on the last occasion, you were pregnant
again.

This time, after the birth of yet another boy, you fell so ill that
almost nothing was to remain in your mind either of the birth
or the period after it. All you could recollect was what you
thought of as 'the circling'. Whenever you opened your eyes it
seemed to you that a dark, vertical grinding or turning, like that

of a water-wheel, was constantly taking place on both sides of whatever you looked at, on the very edges of your vision; when you closed your eyes to escape from this, the whole world began to turn horizontally, with your prostrate body as its very axis. Relief came only in those periods – minutes or entire days, how could you tell? – when you knew nothing. Later you were to be told that during those periods of absence you had in fact babbled and groaned and tried over and over again to get out of bed and go 'home'. There was no persuading you that the house you were in was now your home, the right place for you to be. Listening with wonder and incredulity to this tale you could not have imagined that the day would come when you would think of that 'circling' as a chance that had passed you by. It could so easily have rolled you forever into the darkness and silence you had visited then, where not even your own babblings had been heard by you.

Had you known that your illness had made it impossible for you to have more children, the years that followed would not have been haunted by the fear of another pregnancy and childbirth. In the meantime, there were your three fine boys, all growing, all healthy, to be a source of self-esteem for you and for the village to admire. Three boys were a respectable tally. You had done your duty by your husband and his family. Your life was filled with the lives that had been composed, one by one, within you.

When your husband worked about the house or outside it, he was never to be disturbed; the children learned that early. They learned early, too, that your work was precisely to *be* disturbed. You had to help tend the fields, carry water, gather fuel, bake bread, pick herbs and wild fruit, wash clothes, spin flax; there was no end to your duties. But the children knew that, above all, your job, your function in life, was to be available to them. You did not reproach them for this and you did not repine at it; how could you? What other arrangement was imaginable?

Third
WH SMITH NOTEBOOK

If you had been asked, before you set out on that journey, which member of your family you were most anxious about, you would probably have pointed not at any of the children, but at your husband. Why him? The answer was simple: because of *his* anxieties. Outsiders may have seen him as an ageing, frowning man, measured in his speech and severe in his expression, who looked as if he had succeeded in hardening himself against all feeling; you knew him to be the one among you who was haunted by fears he could hardly bring himself to name. Falling boulders, stampeding animals, tainted food, clothes catching fire, murderers or outbreaks of plague on the road . . . The very fact you and the children had so far been spared misfortunes like these made him all the more convinced that they must still be lying in wait; that a debt was accumulating against the family which would one day have to be discharged. If the moment for that payment could not be predicted, it was only because it was predicted at every moment.

That was the form his love for the children took; he had no other. Hence they knew themselves to be a source of misgiving rather than of pleasure to him; when he was away they felt as if a dark or ponderous barrier between themselves and the world had been lifted, and they revelled in the freedom of it. Then the sense of open space suddenly available to them would fill them with alarm, the younger ones especially, and they would long for him to return.

All this was normal, of course; special to him, to you, to the children; but also perfectly normal, part of what made you know yourselves as a family, a single group, living by its own half-secret rules and habits. Like all other families, in short, each of which had its own such rules and habits, and in just that measure was also different from every other.

So you set off: father, mother, three boys, a single mule to carry your belongings. Do you remember? Of course you do. None of it, from the first day to the last, was to be forgotten; from the scramble down the pass, just a few miles from your village, to the toilsome climb up it – so changed! – weeks later.

The countryside broke open there, at that pass; it was there that the land you lived on revealed itself, for all the weight of its aspiring hills and fields of tumbled basalt, to be nothing more than a great shelf standing out haphazardly in space. Far below it was the floor of the valley, tilted at an angle from north-west to south-east, with its own protrusions and vague declivities; immediately below, the defile you had to thread. Who makes such shelves and floors and fixes them in place? Like a track worn down by ants you could see the path you would have to take across the valley; you could even see some ant-like creatures moving along it here and there. Strange to think that those creatures were really no different from the travellers nearby, each of whom had his own expression and clothes and possessions. You would have found it hard to say who among them were labouring more – the groups straining upwards, men, animals, porters burdened like animals, their mouths open, their eyes bulging with the effort of overcoming the downward pull felt not just by them but by every stone in the pathway; or those like yourselves, going down, who had to resist being overwhelmed by that same pull. The valley, waiting below, seemed to wheel, to shift, to hide and reveal itself around every cleft you passed through, every buttress or shoulder you slowly approached, skirted, and left behind.

Patches of green could be glimpsed down there, and marshy grey, and tarnished silver where fields for sown crops had been scratched into place after the first rains. Everywhere rocks were piled mercilessly on one another, in stacks or folds or scab-like encrustations. All burned with a bluish tint in the sunlight, as if a secret smoke, a smoke you could never see directly, were rising from them. Mingled with human cries were the sounds of bird song, wind whisper, animal grunt and bray, the clatter of dislodged stones, the grinding of sand under the feet of men and beasts alike.

At last it was done. The pass had been negotiated. All the families from the village who were doing the journey together stopped immediately for a meal and a rest. Now you could look back and see those travellers who were still struggling up or down the pass, as you had done; you could marvel at how little difference that great falling-away of the earth made to the dark-bodied birds overhead. To them it did not matter whether they fluttered just above some bushy spur on the cliffside or, barely a wingbeat later, hung hundreds of feet above the valley.

Many more halts like that first one were made over the following days. This or that family would consult with another about when or where to make the next stop; the word would be passed on; the appointed stream or tree or group of huts reached. Mats were spread out on the ground, fires set, meagre meals taken of dates and olives, flat bread and curded cheese. Afterwards, the men, your husband among them, would stretch themselves out on the ground; like the other women, you remained half-seated, half-lying, with your back against a boulder or tree-trunk, the better to keep an eye on the children, or to persuade them that you were keeping an eye on them. They found it harder to rest; now that the break with home and the danger of the descent was behind them, they could afford to be bolder and to range about, showing off to one another, courting little perils, then hastening back for reassurance. Sometimes they played games with sticks, or tried to catch field mice and lizards, or built tiny houses of stone and guarded them against all comers. The weather was mild, the spring air soft, the sun genial, almost as if it were looking at the travellers with a considerately averted gaze. Yet it was always too warm to travel in the middle of the day.

A family like any other; a journey like any other. When you or one of the children was especially tired you would clamber on the mule; for the rest, the soles of your feet registered the softness or hardness of every yard of the way. There seemed no end to the hills or to the road that wound its way between them. Rising more steeply than those you were familiar with from home, and even more littered with boulders, the hills threw their shadows over one another's laps; they cut the sky into ever-changing segments; the heaps and sheaves of rock on them resembled a crop that had been harvested by some unknown race of beings and was ready now to be carried home. Occasionally small groups of soldiers belonging to the army of occupation marched by, moving north or south; then travellers like yourselves drew aside in silence to let them pass; even the children fell silent, guiltily conscious of the attraction these foreign, armoured, beplumed, disciplined men had for them. The people of the country, the half-alien locals, made no trouble for you or for the soldiers. They worked in their tiny fields or sat in front of huts perched on hillsides and straggling along the battered roadway. At night their villages provided shelter; whatever they charged, whatever they felt about their guests, it was safer among them than it would have been out in the fields, exposed to bandits, to wild animals, to the fanatics who had declared the occupied capital and a temple desecrated by the presence of foreign soldiers to be out of bounds.

At last the city could be seen on the high horizon. Tiny at that distance, silver and pale brown in colour, the cube-like buildings gleamed under a stormy sky. The darker the clouds and the greater the confusion in which they were piled together, the more brightly the city shone. Clinging to the summits of its hills, it looked dislodgeable, or crushable, as if the buildings had been scattered there from above, like salt, and could be swept away by an impatient hand.

A last night was spent outside the walls. Rain fell steadily throughout it; the darkness never ceased to whisper and creak and murmur. Silence came only at dawn. By noon the clouds had gone; the sky looked not just clear but rinsed out; every cut or splintered edge of stone in the city walls shone with its own light; underfoot there was a mess of mud, puddles, dribbles, broken reflections. With much noise and irritation people thronged to pay the tolls demanded of them as they and their animals passed through the gates. The smell of wet hides was strong in the air. Together with a dozen others you and your family were jostled through. With the younger children holding your hands, and the older boy holding his father's, you plunged into the lanes and alleyways that would lead you to the house of your husband's kinsmen. They were to be your hosts until the festival was over. By way of gifts you had brought with you food and reeds for plaiting into mats and an earthenware pot. You would all sleep in the courtyard of their house, unless the rain drove you indoors.

There are no wonders to report. Only facts. Just what happened. The wonders are in the facts, if they are to be found anywhere; there is nowhere else from which they can show themselves or in which they can remain hidden. Nothing can be special unless it is ordinary too: how else, being what we are, could we recognise it?

This has to be true of your oldest son, too. You did not dwell especially on the differences between him and other boys of his age. There was no reason for you to do so. Of course he was like the others. Of course he was different to you. Any mother would say that about any of her children. By now you took it for granted that you should think of him as being more intense by nature than his brothers. The stare of his green-gold eyes and the slight frown between them had always told you as much; so had the tilt of his head, his slightly awkward stride, even the slow, distinctive, cat-like blinking that had invariably been a sign from infancy onwards that he was about to fall asleep.

While the younger ones could never get close enough to you, in bed or out of it, he could not bear such intimacies. They affected him as you had seen some domestic animals affected by a human touch or approach: though they might need it, it made them uneasy, shrinking, even wincing in demeanour. He had always been like that; at any rate once the plumpness and simplicity of infancy was behind him.

And his mind? His spirit? But you know that that is exactly what I am talking about! Could a mother, of all people, know her child's spirit without knowing his wrists and ankles, his neck and the point of hair that grew down into the hollow at the back of it, his postures, the turns of his head, the movement of his eyes and eyelids? Even when he was hurt, when he had grazed or cut himself, he could hardly wait for your ministrations, whatever they were, to be over, so that he could be left alone with his pain, to get on with it, to suffer it and be healed from it in his own fashion. If one speaks of that, is one referring to his mind or his body? To the child or the man? The beginning or the end?

Yes, he was clever. He learned to read well before most children who attempted the task. He sang beautifully. Naturally you were proud of these attainments, as any parent would have been. He did not show any signs of exceptional piety, or exceptional kindliness, or exceptional curiosity about the reasons for God's actions, the whereabouts of the dead, our right to slaughter sheep and eat their flesh, the nature of pain, why soldiers came and scourged a group of rebels in the central square of the village, until their screams turned to groans and their groans to silence and they were spreadeagled against the sky like birds whose wings would never come together again; birds that were rags when they were later brought down. He trembled when he saw such things, and ran from them; when he saw a dog with its jaw broken by a stone, or the madwoman with a goitre pointed a finger at it and shouted out his name as if she held him responsible for her condition; he trembled and changed colour, his heart beat so fiercely it became visible in his throat. But you yourself went through the same, or something like it, at such sights and on such occasions; so did his brothers; so did half the villagers. How many of them, after certain recurring events, punishments, fights, even illnesses, had difficulty in meeting one another's eyes, knowing what those eyes had seen.

So he was like the rest of them, or enough of them; different only, always, in being more aloof. He did not cry like his brothers, or bury his head in your lap, as they did; when he had bad dreams, and was woken by them, he did not cling to you as the others did; as even his father did. Instead he gazed unseeingly at you, where you stood or kneeled above him; he moved his lips but produced no sounds, compelled to wait bewilderingly for a return of order, of a connection between himself and what he finally recognised to be around him; then he would turn away.

Well, the days he and you and the others had together in the capital went by. Like all the provincials who had come to town for the festival, you stood in the courtyard of the temple at the appropriate times. Obscured from the view of insignificant people like yourselves, the priests and their acolytes went about their business. There was some chanting, a few processions, the exchange of many rumours of alarming or promising omens. Men and women traded goods and opinions. Festive meals were eaten in family groups and children fell asleep in makeshift beds and at unaccustomed hours. The time to go drew closer. When you tried later to reconstruct those days, as you found yourself doing over and over again – looking in them for some explanation for what was to happen, some hint of it, some key to it, some point you could seize and thus wrench days and events back to what they should have been – it seemed to you that all sorts of random impressions came back in a tumult, but never that which you were looking for. Faces, expressions, buildings, the grittiness of a paving slab under-foot, tilted shadows, chickens in a basketwork coop, grapes, sleeves, voices, words . . . and beneath them or within them, nothing. Emptiness. An eternal incredulity.

This is what happened. Your oldest son and his friend, a boy from one of the families that had accompanied you on the pilgrimage, devised between them a little scheme or diversion. The suggestion they made was simple enough. The friend's family was leaving for home two days before you had planned your departure. Instead of waiting and leaving with you, your son asked if he could go with his friend. The other family had children even younger than yours, so they would be travelling slowly. You would overtake them soon enough. Then the whole party would travel on together. The friend's family, the boys told you, had already been asked and had said they were quite agreeable. Now it was your turn.

Eyes fraught with hope, foreheads tense at the prospect of the adventure ahead of them, the two boys waited for your answer. How could you turn them down? The friend's family were fellow-townsmen, long known to you. The proposed arrangement was to be a part of the youngsters' holiday, different from all that had gone before, something for them both to remember. You had no choice but to agree.

Your son had never yet been away from his parents overnight. He was so excited, the night before, he found it difficult to sleep. In the morning you packed food for him; you told him to be careful; standing outside the house, holding his cusp-like shoulders in your hands, you gave him the kiss he was kind enough not to flinch from. On his lips there was a small, nervous smile which seemed to have pushed or dug itself into the skin around them. No one else was in the lane. The younger children were still asleep; their father had made his abrupt farewell inside. The sun had yet to rise. The marks of yesterday's feet were imprinted in the dust of the lane. Despite his aloofness, or because of his aloofness, you had always felt this boy to be more keenly yours, or more vulnerably yours, than the others. Perhaps you loved the younger ones better because you felt less tense about them, less watchful or constricted. No matter. He was the first for you, the pathbreaker; he always would be.

And of none of it could you say a word! Only, 'You must be careful' and (trying to meet his smile with one of your own) 'It'll be nice to see you again.' Mothers have always said such things to their departing sons; just as their sons have always done their best to hide what it cost them to go. Nevertheless, one by one, they have gone. Looking into his face, and afterwards at his retreating, bravely unconcerned shoulders, you were not troubled by any of his father's excruciatingly exact forebodings. You did not really worry about what the world might do to him. It was the thought of what he might do to himself you could not bear. He turned the corner. The lane was empty. The roof edges began to quiver. The sun was rising.

Two days later you came to the place appointed for your meeting with him and the family with whom he had gone. The family was waiting there, as arranged. But your boy was not with them. He had never been with them. They had not seen him. He had not come to the house at the stipulated time. They had waited for him, and then set out, assuming that he had changed his mind at the last moment, or that his parents had changed it for him.

All this they stammered out in a moment in a few phrases. Your husband said not a word; he chewed with a sideways movement on his back teeth; in his eyes there was the dawn of a recognition or acknowledgement which, even in that moment, with your blood beating up in your head in fierce irregular darkenings, *you* recognised. So! This was how it had come! He had *told* you it would come! You turned your eyes from him and looked back the way you had travelled, as if the boy were bound to be following immediately behind you. No one was there. You shouted out his name. No one replied. You fell to the ground. No one moved to lift you from it.

In the end it was your husband who decided what was to be done. Your friends agreed to wait by the roadside with the two younger children and the mule; he and you would go back to the city to look for the missing boy. The children, already in tears because their brother had disappeared, and because their parents were in such a distraught state, cried out more loudly still on learning they were to be left with strangers. But your husband was not to be dissuaded. The two of you turned back. Footsore, speechless, unable to look at one another, you hurried through a world that was full to bursting, full to madness, with manifestations or appearances of all kinds, and yet utterly empty of meaning.

Let us not imagine that this boy was to be found cheerfully instructing the elders at the temple. Not this one. He was not there. He was not to be found anywhere. He was not with your kinsmen. He was gone. You searched for him in the streets and markets, in the temple quarter, in the houses of everyone you knew in the city; you asked the guards at the gates; you went to the priests and the civil magistrates. None of the people you approached had anything to tell you. Some were sympathetic, most indifferent, a few suspicious, a few roused to a pitying but not unpleasureable curiosity. Days later, your faces and voices changed from what they had been before, you and your husband returned to your remaining children.

Fourth
WH SMITH NOTEBOOK

You would not stop looking for him. Your staring, listening air became as much a part of you as your prominent eyes or the veins that showed in your neck and hands. You could not bear to be parted from your remaining children; if they were gone for more than an hour or two you would become uneasy and restless, and then set out to look for them. They never became used to the embarrassment of your coming after them, or waiting for them at a distance, or hastening back home, as if by coincidence, once you saw them turned in that direction. Yet it was not they – and they knew it all too well – who were the objects of the furtive eagerness and expectancy you betrayed on your return to the house, even when you had been away for minutes only.

It maddened your husband to see it. In vain for him to shout that the boy was lost, gone, dead, stolen, taken away by desert people to be kept as a slave or to be sold as a slave, finished. He had said the prayers for the dead. There was nothing more to be done.

As if he had made his peace with what had happened! As if he had forgiven you for letting the boy go that morning! He never looked at you but you saw a double reproach in his eyes: for having done what you had then; for having become what you were now. For his sake, and for the sake of the children, you tried as hard as you could to keep to yourself how much of your life was preoccupied with the thought of that lost boy. Or with what amounted to the same thing: the thought of his return.

You failed, of course. Your manner had become your body, and your body betrayed you to them at every move it made. But not even they knew that the loss of that boy and his return were the subject of a reverie which seldom left you. Even in your sleep it did not leave you. Again and again in your dreams you and your son were reunited. Sometimes he came in horrible or frightening forms, like an animal, perhaps, or an old man, or a stone grown mysteriously animate; but you always knew him at once, and greeted him, and he always acknowledged his identity to you. Even when his words denied it, he made that acknowledgement in secret ways, known only to you. There were also rare, simple dreams in which you were happy together, as though no parting had ever taken place. Sometimes, worst of all perhaps, he was just as he had been when you had last seen him, only hostile or indifferent, preparing interminably to set off on some journey on which he would not allow you to accompany him. Occasionally, whether as boy or man or tame bird, whether faceless or wearing the face of someone else in the village, he blamed you for his disappearance: why had you allowed it to happen, why hadn't you looked after him properly, it was all your fault. From such nightmares you would wake up only to wish yourself directly back into them, for nothing was worse than the nightmare of waking to know once again that he was indeed gone and that you were where you had been before. How much better off you would have been if you had known him to be dead!

So another day would begin. In winter it rained; in spring the grass was starred with tiny wild lupins, white and pale blue in colour, yellow trefoil, the scarlet cups of anemones, cyclamens that swept their petals back like wings; then the summer scorched them away, as if with disdain, knowing itself to be king of this climate, the one who would rule longest and most fiercely. Whatever the season, whatever the activities around the house or in the village that kept you busy, each day followed an unvarying pattern. From the moment of waking a kind of game began which you played with time or which time played with you. Its name was hope. It never varied in form, this game; not in any significant fashion. You had no choice as to whether or not you should play it. When you woke in the morning, hope was minimal, virtually indistinguishable from despair; as the day wore on it would grow stronger, by imperceptible stages; it would assert itself most strongly, no matter how much you resisted it, or all the more firmly because you resisted it, just before nightfall. The simplest form it took was that of a direct expectation or conviction that you were about to see your son. It might be just as you were busy slapping dough into shape; then you would try to think where you would put your flour-covered hands. Or it might be when you walked down the lane and imagined him to be just around this corner or that; or when you went to the edge of the village and found yourself expecting him to cross that field towards you, or to emerge from behind that tree, or from behind those rocks – now, now, now.

No. Not now.

Other forms assumed by hope were of a more elaborate kind. A man was on his way to you with a cryptic message which only you could understand; it was necessary, therefore, for you to watch out not for your son but for that mysterious messenger. Or word would come from the authorities: an official would knock on the door one day, bearing in his hand a letter telling you where to go and when to go there in order to meet your son. Or he himself would return just as you were about to eat the midday meal three days hence. As the next sabbath was about to begin. When the sabbath ended. When you got home after having been away for the day. When you had managed to compel yourself *not* to expect anything. It would happen if you steeled yourself to leave the house, leave the children, and wander about the hills for a week, on your own; when you came back, he would be waiting for you. Then you would have become the wanderer, he the one sitting impatiently at home, and you would both laugh at that reversal of role. You would go to the capital and find him there, in an exact but on this occasion fulfilled re-enactment of your very first search for him. You would solemnly forswear expecting him between now and some date you would fix upon in the future; you would give an oath of abstention and be true to it – and why, who could tell, just because you had given that undertaking and had shown yourself capable of sticking to it, because you were expecting nothing in the interim, had made up your mind on the matter, had ceased to think of him, had your back turned to him, why, then he might come creeping up to you. . . .

Dusk gave way inexorably to night, light flared and darkened behind the hills, hope dwindled, another day had turned into a disappointment, into nothing. Strangely enough, though, this nothingness was in itself not as painful as waking in the morning and knowing that the game of hope and despair was about to begin all over again. At night you would know quite firmly, without doubt or ambiguity, that the day just over had not been the day you were waiting for; it never had been the day; it had been wrong for you to suppose that it might be. It followed, therefore, that you were bound to be one day nearer the real or true day. Also, provided you managed to sleep, which you usually did, the nights went by more quickly than the hours of daylight, and when you slept there was the chance that you might dream of his coming.

For how long is it possible for someone to go on like this? For how long can you go on playing this game, or being played by it? Go on with it while cooking, washing, talking, helping to bring in the meagre harvest, salting meat, nursing other women in childbed, travelling shorter or longer distances to see relatives, gathering firewood, spinning yarn, scolding the children or looking after them during their illnesses? The answer slowly came home to you over the years. You could go on for years! For a lifetime! For ever! You could try to hide from others what you were doing; you could try to hide it from yourself; you could try a hundred, a thousand times to put a stop to it (and try also, as you did so, not to make some secret, half-magical ritual out of your renunciation, and thus to continue to hope by other means, as it were); you could try fiercely, try wearily, try out of a sick tedium, try out of fear of what would become of you if you did not succeed – and then find that you were still doing it and that what you were doing in the imagined secrecy of your head was more or less suspected by everyone around you.

There were other, outside sources of help available to people in distress, and those too you consulted. You heard about old women in the neighbourhood, or further afield, who would use the spells and charms they had at their command to tell you what had become of your missing boy; they would find him for you or enable you to find him; at least, they would stop you thinking about him. There were wandering healers and holy men who could do the same. You went to them all, and still the boy remained missing and still his absence filled your life and emptied it. There were also women and men – and children – in the village and outside it who said that you were crazy, that you yourself were a witch; they teased your two boys and sneered at your husband and made jests directly to you which appeared to amuse them. They told you that your son had come back, taken one look at you and run away again. That he had been dressed up like a soldier or a king. That he lived in the clouds or on the moon.

Even your own children jeered at you sometimes. They never referred directly to what was ailing you; that was impossible for them, both because of your pain and theirs. Instead they called you a dreamer or a sleepwalker and scornfully asked you what day of the week you thought it was or what month of the year. As they grew older they also showed their resentment simply by staying away from home for longer and longer intervals, even though they knew the anguish this caused you. They were not hard-hearted boys; far from it; it filled you with remorse whenever you saw how unmistakably waif-like they sometimes appeared to be; how anxious and exposed, almost as if their parents had died at an early age and they had never entirely recovered from the blow. The irony of it did not escape you. This was especially true of the older boy, who had had to assume more than the ordinary burden of responsibility carried by a first-born son. Like their father, the boys had suffered doubly: first their brother had been taken from them; then they had lost all that their mother might otherwise have been to them.

But knowing this was merely to know it; it changed nothing. Outside the village there was a particular group of boulders which for you were always charged with the presence of your lost son, indeed which you thought of as 'his', simply because among them you had once felt with a special intensity that he was about to return to you. There was a bend in the stream running down the hillside which was also his; there, one day, while washing clothes, you had sat back and waited almost calmly for his reflection to appear in the water below you. There were even branches of trees, or patches on tree-trunks, that had, over the years, become his. Emerging from some waking dream of his return – during which you had been telling him exactly what you had been going through at that very moment, as if it were all now safely in the past – emerging from such a dream, you had found yourself staring fixedly at these branches or tree-trunks; thereafter he had taken possession of them, he spoke to you through them.

So the years went by. The children grew up; after what was an age in its passing and a blink of an eye in recollection, they were no longer boys but young men. You remained where you were: trapped in a labyrinth of mourning that was also an expectancy; a condition that was at one and the same time claustrophobically tiny and repetitive, and yet also never-ending, as big as the world, co-extensive with everything inside and outside you. Still you laboured, with all your will and in despite of your will, at the task of undoing time, rolling it back, putting it into reverse. But the time that was in fact undone was only and always the present, that which you were actually living through, moment by moment: literally your life-time. Occasionally, with an inexorable repetitiveness of its own, a strange sequence of thoughts about the life you had led would pass through your mind. It went like this. First: if you could have known when you lost your son that you would be feeling *this* so many years later, you would surely have put an end to yourself. Then: but that was absurd, for you would never have believed it would be possible for you, for anyone, to remain in such a state for so long; the idea of it, let alone the prospect of it, would have been utterly inconceivable to you. Finally: so the years had made this difference at least – once you would have thought such a life to be impossible; now you knew it to be not only possible, but to have been your own, the only one you would ever have! All those years had been reduced to nothing, to smoke – a house of smoke, a family of smoke, work of smoke – by a single thought, or image, or fixed, insensate emotion.

Then, at some indeterminate point of time, you became

aware that the years had after all made a further difference. Though your manias were the same, and would always be the same, it was as if you now went through them, or they went through you, by rote, mechanically, virtually without demanding your attention. They were no longer a cause of alarm or despair to you, but simply what you were to your own consciousness, the way you knew yourself to be the person you were. Every obsessive thought, no matter how stale it was, had once had the mysterious power of seeming to make a cruelly new or fresh groove in your mind or flesh each time it appeared. But not now. Now such thoughts came and went almost, as it were, on their own. You perceived them, you recognised them, but you did not feel them.

Thereafter you occasionally found yourself able to remember what it was like to have loved the boy before you had known that you had lost him. How close to you was that emotion still; how distant or ignorant the girl who had felt it.

Fifth
WH SMITH NOTEBOOK

Then you found him.

Or so you believed.

The circumstances were commonplace enough. You had been with your older son to a village some distance from your own. He had had business to transact there and you had gone along to keep him company. Now it was time to start the trek home, across the bald hillsides. Just as you were about to leave, however, he had been attracted to the crowd gathering around a pedlar or healer who had begun to put on his show in the centre of the village. Such people were a familiar enough sight in your part of the world: the countryside abounded with itinerant jugglers, magicians, shamans, layers-on of hands, expounders of God's word, whippers-up of rebellion against the occupying power and their local collaborators, prophets who spoke with a confident intimacy of terrible and glorious events in the offing. Some travelled with small groups of followers; some had connections with bands of rebels who hid in inaccessible places; some were solitaries. None of them, none of the words they uttered, meant anything to you; not any longer. In your misery you had sought help from some of them, and all had let you down. So why should you pay any attention to this one?

You did not follow your son as he made his way to the edge of the crowd. Seated on the ground, with your back against a low stone wall, your knees drawn up in front of you, your hands clasped just below them, your face turned to the sun that had already begun to decline towards the shadowed, gleaming, roughly rounded tops of the westernmost hills, you waited patiently and incuriously for his return. The village was one you had not visited before, but every sound that came to your ears – the bark of every dog, the trailing, complaining call of every fowl to its companions, the cry or cough of every child, even the scuffling of the feet of the crowd – was known to you. So was the faint, challenging voice of the mendicant in the distance, as he struggled to hold the attention of his audience, and the occasional murmur of its response. People were always coming together in search of diversion and some kind of enlightenment; terror too. How well you knew their ways. You were an old woman now, or felt yourself to be one; all that was youthful about you was the shame of your incompleteness, of having lived not by what you had done, but in a dream of what you had missed.

The voices grew louder. The subdued clamour was meaningless, like something heard or imagined as sleep approached. You did not turn your head to look at the group until you realised how close it had come. Now it was almost on you. It was not a large one: perhaps twenty, thirty people in all, children included. For some reason the throng opened up momentarily as you looked up. The man at the centre of it glanced in your direction.

What happened then was the same and yet unutterably different from your years of imagining how it might be. It was the same because of the unerring certainty that split your heart. It was as if his gaze had not gone through your eyes at all, but directly there, to the one place within you that could not be mistaken. You had always been convinced that you would know at once, if ever the chance were given to you; and look, you had been right.

So the moment came as you had dreamed of its coming. Yet it was also utterly unlike your imaginings. It was *not* an imagining, and that was the greatest difference of all. It was not eroded from within by darkness, by dream-incertitudes and dream-distortions. How vivid those dreams had seemed to you, when you had been afflicted by them; and how inconsequential, what wisps of mind, you now knew them to be. It was daylight here; there were bodies casting shadows on the ground; the pressure of a stone wall was rigid against your back. Everything was in its place. None of it could be other than it was. All the other possibilities that had tormented you for so long were excluded, forever. They went out of you in a single convulsion, in one swarm or spasm. The freedom of being without them! Of being part of what had to be!

Then, or in the same moment, you knew another difference, which was almost as great. You had always anticipated that the moment of recognition would be one of tumult and tears. You would call out, take him round the neck, shake him, look into his eyes, tell him who you were and who he was, compel him against his will or understanding to go through his own convulsion of acceptance. A part of him that had been fractured years before, and had then stiffened, congealed, been sealed over, would be broken anew; feeling would burst like blood through arteries and tissues long dry and dead. What agony that would be! How he would cry out at it! He would cry so loudly that people would come running at the noise, and point and stare and shove at one another to get closer to the heart of whatever they imagined to be happening.

Instead of which the moment came and went in silence. You remained motionless. Perhaps some sound escaped from your breast; if it did, you did not know what it was. The exchange of glances between you and him had been so brief it could not have been noticed by anyone other than yourself; by him perhaps least of all. It had been nothing and had done nothing, other than change your life. You continued to sit where you had been, staring as if from a child's height at the backs of legs and sandalled feet, the hems of garments. Even the grains of sand pushed into glittering little heaps or flattened under people's feet were visible to you. So much was to be seen out there, it was not to be borne. Covering your face with your hands you waited – for what you did not know – dark, unshed tears welling up within you.

The touch of his hand on your shoulder could not have been lighter or more delicate. There was no need for you to look up to make sure it was indeed his touch you had felt; you simply put your hand over his, in a fierce gesture. The last time the two of you had been together you had held him by his shoulders. Now the circle was complete.

Intimately, almost caressively, the man said something to you about how much you had suffered. His voice was like that of more than one man: it ran deep, yet high notes glinted and twinkled at random within it. For the benefit of the crowd he repeated what he had just said; he hardly seemed to speak more loudly than before, yet his voice itself told you that everyone, even those farthest from him, would hear him without difficulty. An arm encircled your shoulders and you felt yourself being pulled to your feet. It was impossible to resist. When you opened your eyes all you saw for the moment was the flash of his, so close to you; within each gold iris was a tiny, unmoving circle of darkness, like a perfect pit or well-mouth. Then his hand came over your brow: the weight of his other hand rested on your head. Your broken heart, you were told, was healed. You would go home at peace with yourself.

The dark weight of the hand over your eyes was removed. The man in front of you – thin, bearded, long-haired – was smiling faintly. His lips were dry, broken by cracks into living segments; his eyes were darker than those you had stared into more than two decades before, in the early-morning, smoke-tainted air of a quiet city alleyway. Then you had looked down into his eyes; now you had to look up at them. At their corners were many fine lines; deeper lines ran across his sun-darkened brow. His hair was darkened too; only the very fringes of his beard were still the light colour of the boy's hair, as you remembered it. The wonder with which you gazed at him was also a complete certainty; without that certainty there would have been nothing to wonder at.

So, at last, his name emerged from your lips. As you uttered it, it turned into a claim and a cry of joy. Yes, joy: for the first time since you had seen him exultation swept through you and flung you towards him. They would never take you from him now!

Still smiling remotely, unsurprised by your assault, apparently unaffected by the name you had given him, he backed away, warding you off with an uplifted hand. Then he withdrew from you in more dramatic fashion. One moment he was retreating from you; the next he had begun a dance in the midst of the crowd. Skipping, shaking, wagging his head and shoulders, he let his feet go ahead of him in a kind of rapid pattering or beating on the ground, like nimble hands on a drum. People crowded forward more closely to see what was going on; others jostled back, to get out of his way. There was some laughter, one or two boys on the outskirts of the crowd began capering in imitation. Without pause or warning, as if nothing were easier than to control his breath while his whole body swirled about and his feet beat their rhythm on the ground, he put back his head and began to chant wordlessly. The sound was like an endless ribbon emerging from his throat, with every now and again a fold or doubling-over in it, where two notes seemed to run together before the one that had been there gave way to its usurper. His shoulders rose and fell, his hands weaved patterns in the air, his feet drummed merrily and unpredictably on the ground. Still the chant came from him. It was like music, like speech, like a bird or an animals's cry, like something more tangible than any of these; and was none of them. On and on it went. His face raised to the sky, he sang to the sky, not to the people around him, and they listened all the more intently to him just for that reason.

In mid-note, in mid-step, as abruptly as he had begun, he ceased. A noise from the crowd, half-admiring, half an expression of puzzlement at the sudden conclusion to the perform-

ance, broke the silence that followed. The man made his way
through the group and began walking, on his own, across the
square, towards the low, stone houses on the far side and the
open country beyond. He did not look behind him. Apparently
he was finished, indifferent to the response of his audience; the
whim or imperative that had uttered itself through his singing
and dancing now exhausted.

Was that all? What had been done? What had been the lesson
of his visit? The benefit of it? Had he brought consolation or
mockery? The villagers gazed at each other, as if wondering
who had been the more exposed to scorn by the anti-climax of
the man's departure: he or themselves. Everything was as it had
been. The only change was that the sun was now closer to the
hills than before. There was no breeze, yet a ripple of adjust-
ment of some kind seemed to be on the move through the
cooling, suddenly grainy, golden air. Unabashed, the man's
helper went among the group, trying to sell charms which
would keep away a variety of ills. Rounded green stones
intricately veined with black, these were, like an internal organ
from a slaughtered animal.

As the people dispersed you were joined by the son who had
brought you there. His expression was perturbed. He had heard
you shout out his brother's name, but the idea that you might
have been greeting the man, hailing or claiming him by that
name, did not occur to him. How could it? You looked in the
direction the man had taken. There he was, on the eastern side

of the village, a solitary figure in a brown tunic, passing beyond the last of the houses. He was carrying nothing; not even a staff; not even a bag of bread.

That walk! You could not be mistaken about him. Not when you had again and again given up waiting, only to be relentlessly taken up by waiting; not when you had schooled yourself never to expect anything of your own expectations; not when you had come to hate so much your own hopes. With a strangely dismissive, admonitory gesture you turned away from your son; you had nothing to say to him. The one you now had to get hold of was this salesman, the helper, the pedlar of stones.

He was a small, swarthy, bent creature, raggedly dressed, much older than his master, with a black, stubble-bearded jaw that was thrust forward and also to one side, in a kind of smile. His lips were pulled tight and yet crumpled within by the curve they were fixed into; and his murky, bluish eyes also ran continually to that side, as if mimicking the deformation below, or vainly attempting to see it. He would dart a look in front of him but it would then slide away, slide down, irresistibly reverting to its corner. He spoke with an unfamiliar accent, hardly moving his twisted lips. No, he did not know his master's name; he did not think his master had a name. No, he did not know where his master came from; from everywhere and nowhere, he thought. No, he did not know where his master was going next; nobody knew; it could be in any direction. It could even be to two places at the same time, his

master was such a great magician. Yes, his master sometimes
had more than one follower, but only when he wanted to; he
could make anyone his follower just by looking at him. No, he
was not going after his master now; he would spend the night
in the village and find him the next day, or the day after.
Where? He did not know; he would be drawn to wherever he
happened to be. And how did his master live, what did he live
on? On air, on water, on God's word, on what he found by the
roadside, on what people gave him, sometimes on nothing at
all.

He was teasing you. A twisted, crouching little man he may
have been, with eyes that could not meet yours and a beggarly
little satchel of stones slung by a band from his shoulder, but he
was letting you know, in his own fashion, that he was more
than a match for your questions and that he despised you for
your curiosity. So this was the confidant or accomplice of the
son you had lost! Let your son's walk or his eyes or his hair be
what they were to you: nevertheless a sense of desolation at the
thought of how little you knew about him, how little you might
mean to him, took possession of you. Perhaps this man was
right. Your son did have no name, no family, no place of origin,
no destination: having once been lost, and lost so many years
before, they could never be retrieved. Then all your dreams
would prove to be even more delusory in being fulfilled than
they had been as torments and deferments.

The villagers had dispersed; the pedlar had turned away from
you with an expression of malignly childish amusement on his

face; your other son pulled at your arm. In the west the sun, suddenly bigger and flatter than it had been all day, and richer in colour too, began to quiver as its rim touched the darkening hill beneath it. Yet another thought of which you had been innocent during all those years of obsession, when you believed yourself to have exhausted every possible conjecture about your son's disappearance, occurred to you. Could it be that the boy you had said goodbye to (the expression of his face already that of someone who was elsewhere, gone from you) – could it be that he had planned his disappearance from the very beginning; that he had not been, like you, the endlessly suffering victim of what had befallen him, but on the contrary its organiser and originator?

Was that possible? You leaned towards your other son, your younger son, who had never been parted from you, and whispered to him the discovery you had made.

Of course he did not believe you. He had suffered too much from you and your mania in the past. He simply picked up the bag in which he had carried the day's provisions for the two of you, and set off home. He did not look behind him. You could follow or not, as you chose.

Sixth
WH SMITH NOTEBOOK

How does a man become aware that he has been summoned to carry out special tasks in the world? Is there any one moment when he knows with utter certainty that he is nothing more (and also nothing less) than the servant of forces greater than himself? If such a moment comes, is he astonished by it or does he feel he has always been waiting for it? Or both at once? Is his inner conviction dependent on the acquiescence of others; or the acquiescence of others dependent on the strength of his conviction; or both at once?

Impossible for you to avoid asking such questions, given the company you were keeping. What you had taken to be a spasm of mockery from your son's follower, when you had first spoken to him, turned out to be nothing of the kind: he might have been quoting from his master. Father, mother, brothers, childhood, home, destination, possessions, memory itself – he would admit to none of these. The preoccupations of other men and women and the limitations which they took for granted (even as they strained against them) meant nothing to him. For him there was no past and no future, only the moment in which he lived and which lived in him. Now. And now. And again now. Now, unendingly. At every moment he began again, or so he said; and the world began with him. The rest was nothing. Where was the past which preoccupied you so much? Where the future? They were less real, less to be taken into account, than this stalk of grass or that bird on a branch. And look, now they too were gone, gone irrevocably, and a new present was upon you. Or rather, a new present *was* you. Just because this present 'you' was always changing, always in flight, it mattered far more than all the supposed fixities and unalterabilities of the past. As for the future, it mattered not at all, for the one who would live through it, whatever forms were taken by it, was not the person you were now. How could you be so concerned with the fate of someone who did not yet exist and might never come into existence?

With words of this kind he was always free. Facts, however, remained not just undivulged, but unrecognised, indistinguishable from random or grotesque speculation. Your tears or pleadings or anger had no effect on him. Perhaps, he might say teasingly at one moment, you were after all his mother: why should you not be? Or perhaps that old woman bent under a load of firewood, there, by the side of the road – she was the one. Or why not that ewe over there? Could that bull be his father? That rock his brother? That stream his sister? Why not? Perhaps he had been suckled by a bear, taught to speak by a fox, shown how to fly by a hawk? It was possible. Anything was possible. What we believed was what actually happened; not the other way around, as timorous and unenlightened souls insisted.

You looked into those tawny, light-filled eyes and saw in them that he would never be prepared to acknowledge that you *meant* your questions; they were not intended to be jokes or merely to serve as provocations for him to indulge himself in his fantasies. He granted you a familiarity, even an intimacy, that cost him nothing and committed him to nothing; a smile that had no warmth, no concern, no curiosity. Were you to leave him he would make no effort to follow you; he would merely cease to think about you, you would be forgotten, dismissed. That was how he was and always would be. If you were to produce incontrovertible proof that he was indeed your son it would not make any difference to him. He would still know himself to be self-begotten, self-reared, self-inspired. Everything and everyone he encountered was equally close to him and equally distant. When he grew old, if he grew old, no matter how wrinkled he became, he would be thin, as he was now, and bearded, and probably poorly clad; his eyes would still gleam slantwise in the sun with a mockery that was a kind of cajolery too; his voice would still be caressive and multiple in its tones, and would still effortlessly flex itself to produce utterances of the same kind as before.

And as he was, so he wished all those around him to be. Or so he claimed. The longer you were with him the more incomprehensible that claim, above all others, seemed to you. The wonders he practised, or pretended to practise, or persuaded others he practised, or merely hinted at, were trivial in comparison. That the world was a place where a man of singular gifts could fly or change his shape or heal the sick or commune with the beasts or spirits – all this was banal when set against the notion that mankind as a whole could be changed by being preached at, by being taught, or even by having an example set before them. That men and women, all men and women, could be talked out of the warring impulses and instincts within them; that through some immense effort of will they could alter forever the drift of their reveries and the habits of their souls; that an inner belief or conviction would enable them to shed their need for identity and continuity; and that they should make such changes their most cherished ambition not just for themselves, or for this person or that, but for everyone, for the entire race – all such notions, which seemed to follow from what he said and from how he lived, remained unintelligible to you. And as unintelligible was the corresponding expectation that people had the capacity to persuade themselves or to be persuaded *into* different states from those to which their experience had habituated them. Were they to talk themselves into blitheness? Indifference? Insouciance? Detachment from past and future?

How much you, of all people, would have wished it to be possible; and how well you, of all people, knew it never could be! Had not your life wasted itself against your will and your will wasted itself against your life? Besides, if what he urged had actually come to pass, what would have been left for your son to do? Then there would have been nobody for him to preach to, nobody to impress with his magic powers and tricks, from healing to juggling, from dancing to speaking in unknown languages. If everyone lived as he did and thought as he did, who would he and his follower have stolen from, and what would people have saved that would have been worth stealing? Who would there have been for him to betray, and to whom would he have betrayed them?

He went into mountains higher and wilder than any you had seen before: barbarously littered with rock outcrop, tufted with stubborn bushes, rent with clefts in which mist unpredictably gathered and dispersed, as if such places were vents through which something hidden and otherwise motionless quietly breathed. He entered villages that seemed to have been ruined rather than built by the people who lived in them, and who, in fear of the evil eye, were especially anxious to conceal their children from his gaze. He crossed tracts of swampland from which herons, with movements as ungainly as their cries, laboured into flight, trailing their legs behind them, while flocks of smaller birds fled like handfuls of grain flung wide. He circled around a lake which you had heard of but never before seen: the level of its still, opaque water seemed higher in the distance than it was immediately below, as if some uncanny power within it enabled it to slope upwards; higher still were pelt-like patches of colour which alone made manifest and gave shape to the haze-shrouded brokenness of the surrounding slopes.

This countryside, far more remote than the one familiar to you, was your son's kingdom: the place he had marked out for himself. His home was in the villages in which he slept, or on the rocky slopes of gorges, or under trees, or in caves. Everywhere he went the little man went with him, carrying the bags for them both; occasionally others would attach themselves to him for brief periods. At almost every halt he put on a performance of some kind, traded charms and thieved, spoke of what was to come, seduced this person or that (women for the most part) to follow him, and then rebuffed them or fled from them.

It was hard for you to admit to yourself what kind of a man he had grown into, this son of yours, whom you had conceived between a groan and a silence on some long-forgotten night, whom you had lost and endlessly mourned over and dreamed of meeting again, whom you had finally come across by chance on an afternoon like any other, in a place like any other. It was harder still to admit that what saved him from outright evil, and kept his disposition, so far as you could make it out, at the level merely of childish or wanton malice, were precisely the virtues he lacked: pertinacity, ambition, even principle. He had ideas, which he urged on others, but these were, if anything, a means of undoing ambition and principle. He used his gifts of voice and hand occasionally for the good of those to whom he brought relief from illness; more often to disconcert or impoverish them; sometimes to his own harm too; always to impress; never to understand.

Hardest of all to accept, perhaps, was that these were among the reasons why you could not leave him. You had long since got over any fascination you might have felt at having your own scruples overturned and derided. You were too old, much too old, for the life you were leading: not just for its physical hardships and dangers, of which there were no end, even without the confrontations with other nomads which you had to endure, or the flights you had sometimes to make from those whose valuables your son had stolen, only to sell them for rubbish at the next halt or the one beyond it. Far worse than these, worse than cold and heat and a never-ending fatigue, were his mockery of you and his indifference to you, his intermittent hectorings, his treating you as if *you*, not he, were the one who was crazy. This was your portion, without taking into account what you had lost that afternoon when you had set off in pursuit of him, leaving your other son to make his way home on his own and to tell his father and brother whatever story he wished when he got there. Gone forever, the lot of them, all you had ever had.

For what? This! This in the present, the forebodings only about what was to come. But that was the point! You had deserted him once before, or he had deserted you, or had been compelled to desert you, and look what had become of you both as a result . . . . Not that you imagined you would be able to save him from the fate, whatever it might be, he was busy bringing on himself; you were far too weak and he was too strong, in his feckless fashion. But this time it would at least not be the catastrophe of ignorance, of not knowing what had occurred.

And beyond or beneath all this, beyond even your buried wish that you had never met him and had continued to live as before, in the miseries that had once been habitual to you, you knew there was something more mysterious and tantalising which held you fast to him. To you the world had always been an alien and incomprehensible place. Its laws could not be fathomed; its reasons for being as it was, or merely for being, could not be perceived; all its manifestations were different forms of exclusion – rocks excluded you, grass excluded you, trees, clouds, the stars that glittered in isolation or swam indistinguishably together, the shapes of mountains and the urgent, blind noises of sheep, even your own appetites and longings, the irretrievability of the past, the silence of the dead, the clamour-to-come of the yet-to-be-born: all were forms of exclusion. You had to deal with them as best you could, like everybody else; but the conviction that they might speak to you and you to them – the stars too! – in a language either side could comprehend was forever beyond your reach.

For him, by contrast, in his fecklessness and caprice, there appeared to be nothing strange about the world, nothing inexplicable or menacing. It was his place. It spoke to him through its infinite variety of voices and he spoke to it in the voices with which he had been endowed. He knew all that it willed; and it knew all he willed. He had no more fear of what it might do to him than he had remorse for what he did to others. Everything that happened had to happen so that the world could be just as it was; everything he did had to be done so that he could be what he was. So how could any of it be feared or regretted or puzzled over?

That, after his long absence, was the strange comfort or invigoration you found in his presence. It did not leave you even when he fell, as he sometimes did, into protracted spells of inertness and silence, during which he lay motionless for days on end wherever he happened to find himself. Then he would get up, making no reference to what had just passed; his voice would at once regain its self-confidently insinuating and in-different tones and he would set off on the march once more.

How could you pit your sense of exclusion against his inward-
ness with the world he lived in; your compunctions against his
callousness; your doubt against his faith; your waverings
against his firmness – or, for that matter, your fixities of feeling
against his waywardness?

Nor were you the only one who felt like this. Almost
everyone he met knew him to be different from themselves. He
was mad, some said. Conceited, others. Dangerous, others. A
fool, others. And others again spoke of him enthusiastically and
yet a little uneasily, afraid of being thought gullible or sen-
timental, as a prophet and healer, a man whose voice undid
them and whose gaze filled them with awe and joy. Even
dizziness. Those were their words. They came to him with their
ailments – ulcers, lumps in their sides or on their faces, limbs
that would no longer obey them – and went from him declaring
how much better they felt, how the pain had left them, how
they would treasure the pebbles or scraps of bark or tiny bits of
parchment on which he had written magic letters. They pressed
coins and food on him; they asked him to pray for husbands
gone on long journeys or sick children or barren women; they
listened intently to his songs and watched reverentially as he
danced in silence, or to the sound of his own voice, or to the
piping of his companion's flute. That the little man might have
been rifling their huts or their pockets while they gazed
elsewhere, or that his master might inform the commander of a
nearby garrison of secrets that had been imparted to him,
remained unknown to them, or was learned too late. Sickened

by such actions, you woke up on many mornings actually hoping that you would find yourself alone, abandoned by him just as you had seen others abandoned – pathetic women with whom he had made rendezvous he had no intention of keeping; men whom he sent way when he tired of them.

But it never happened. He had adopted you. It was his whim, presumably. It pleased him to torment you. Your readiness to be tormented was irresistible. Perhaps he thought you completed the party in some way that would impress the people you met. What had been a travelling pair was now a travelling trio: the magician; the man with a stubbly muzzle for a face; and you, limping along with them, beggarwoman's clothes hanging about your body, head bowed, hair tangled, face blackened, fingernails broken, ankles swollen and chipped. Occasionally you were tempted to interrupt your son when he gathered a crowd around him and began to perform for them or to talk to them about whatever came into his head; not because you wanted to warn them or to denounce him, but simply in order to tell them your story (which was his story too). Then they might see you as something more than an attendant, an unexplained shadow, part of his freak-show. But you never did it.

As for the other member of the trio, the little man, you had soon learned that you had nothing to fear from him. He was not even jealous of you. He accepted you because his master had done so. He was as harmless in his slyness as in his idiocy. He had phases when he incontinently or compulsively repeated the last word or phrase said to him; he was a wolfer of his food, a drunkard intermittently, the source also of shy, abrupt gestures of friendship and compassion towards you. He would invite you to go first into some shelter he had found from the rain; he would, for all the infantile fierceness of his appetite, proffer you food before falling on it himself.

It was only then, when you were the beneficiary of his inept and intense acts of kindness, that you weakened and wanted to cry. Nothing, after the first few weeks, that your son said or failed to say to you ever had this effect on you. Nor did your thoughts of the family you had left behind, without a word, without even enquiring of them from travellers who might have passed through the village.

There were times when you and the little man clung together for warmth under a single covering; he drowsed and muttered and woke at random hours; waking with him, you would see his eye gleaming vacuously; not once however, did he attempt to commit against you anything that you would have thought of as an impropriety, in your other, ancient life. There was simply no danger in him. He was more your friend, indeed, than your son ever would be. When you were ill he was the one who insisted that the three of you rest until you had recovered. All your son would do for you was to cover your eyes with his hand, place the other hand on top of your head, as he had done on that first afternoon, and tell you that you were healed, whole, better once again. It may have worked for the village women, or for some of them; but not for you.

How long this life went on you could not have said: it was always the same, somehow, yet it had no regularities or recurrences. The countryside changed, like the people you met and the villages you passed through, and yet all were indistinguishable from one another. There was no way for you to measure the passage of days; only the seasons were easy to tell apart. It seemed as if this would go on until your death, which sometimes appeared to you to be wonderfully close. You were sure it could not be denied you; it was within reach of your hand; who would begrudge it to you? Then you would find yourself marching on, as strong as you had been at the very beginning, when you had taken the eastward turning out of that village, in the direction that led away from home.

Seventh
WH SMITH NOTEBOOK

I wish you could tell me just one thing, so that I might be spared the task of seeming needlessly to suggest it to you. Did you ever ask yourself if you had erred in claiming the wanderer as your son? Or were you always certain you had been right? Clearly you must often have *wished* you were wrong; but that is not what I have in mind. Even to make such a wish is to reveal the strength of your conviction about his identity and yours. The same would apply to your speculations about how much better off you would have been if you had simply never met him.

No, what I am thinking of are moments of quite another sort. I imagine them coming to you without warning, for no particular reason you could ever make out; perhaps at times when you were not in especial mental or physical discomfort, but merely abstracted or preoccupied or even bored. For example: waking early and waiting for the first signs of a daybreak that would not come. Or glancing unthinkingly towards the west and seeing to your surprise that yet another long day was about to be spectacularly yet silently consigned to the flames. Or, on the march, when there would suddenly appear before your inner eye, with hallucinatory vividness, the memory of a humble household item – a pot, say, or a strap, or a blanket – you had used day after day for years on end, and which you believed you would never hold in your hands again. At such moments did it not occur to you that the connection you had insisted on between yourself and the wanderer might be nothing more than a fanatical figment of your own creation, another manifestation of the dreaming disease which in one form had rotted so much of your life, and which in another had now taken it over entirely? And if such thoughts came to you, in what fashion did you regard them? With wonder? Fear? Unimaginable mirth?

Eighth
WH SMITH NOTEBOOK

Always on the move; eating at irregular intervals; gathering people around him whenever the mood took him; sucking at grass stems or scuffing the dust around his ankles or drinking from cupped hands, like a child; going occasionally on well-kept roads but more often sticking to paths known only to himself; wandering always with an apparent randomness, now heading east, now west, now south, now turning on his tracks and going north again, yet invariably, at the end of each week, finding himself a few miles nearer the capital; beginning at last the long climb towards it, from a low-lying, desert-like area of sand and scrub, through brown and grey hills which only at that time of year were tinged with the faintest green on their westerly slopes; seeing from below, and from far off, the untidy scatter of stone shapes that marked the capital, distinguishable at once from the rocks that crested every other hilltop by the flatness of their surfaces, the rectilinearity of their angles – through all these journeys, through all these accumulating occasions, he underwent a change that was visible to no one but yourself. There was no one else who could have observed it. He was never long enough in any one place for his audiences to see it; as for your own companion, the little man, he was simply incapable of observing his master. He could only watch him, grin at him, mimic him, wait doglike for his orders; judgement was beyond him.

But to you the differences were plain, though you could not have said when you first became conscious of them. He had always regarded the randomness and impulsiveness of his deeds, even their whimsicality, as evidence of his superiority to all those who did not dare to act as he did. That conviction had in itself been his greatest strength. Now it was different. Now it was as if he had begun to fear that he might find himself the victim as well as the perpetrator of his own actions. Something had happened or was happening within him which he had no hope of turning to his own advantage; and he knew it. From time to time you caught on his face a look of bewilderment and helplessness it had never worn before. Nothing reminded you more of the son you had lost than that look; it was so youthful and self-doubting.

Yet the only effect of such moments of dismay was to make his behaviour even wilder and more reckless subsequently. His exhortations to the crowds he gathered around him dwelt more and more obsessively on blood, storms, standings still of the sun, dippings of the moon, fallings apart of stone from stone, plagues, fires, voices, wars. His dances and songs became more frenzied than before; sometimes they would end in a kind of convulsion, when foam appeared on his lips, his eyes rolled back, his hands and feet twitched, his breath gargled like liquid in his throat. He found new ways of using his conjuring tricks to humiliate members of his audiences; he jeered at them; he thieved more openly from them; offering to heal the maimed or sick among them he would whisper in their ears that they were finished, that they would be better off dead. Forgetting his own acts of betrayal and collaboration with the country's foreign rulers, he began openly to incite his listeners to attack them. They were scum, he said, an alien defilement; their soldiers were vermin to be hunted and killed whenever the opportunity arose. The fact that he knew nothing about the loyalties of his listeners did not restrain him, nor did their lowered eyes, their shuffling feet, their sidling movements away from one another, as if they were only accidentally hearing such things.

Away from crowds, alone with you and his companion, out in the fields or roadways, he swung between rage and an equally frenzied good humour. One moment he might be embracing the little man, the next hitting him with his fists, kicking him where he lay on the ground, leaving him to curse or cry or settle into a steady snivelling that could go on for hours at a time. You came in for your share, too, of pushes and curses. Now it was for getting in his way, now for failing to hear something he had said, now for not having food ready when he asked for it. He held you up to ridicule in front of his audiences. You were a foolish, pathetic woman who claimed to be his mother, and who followed him about the country for that reason; but he knew you were nothing of the kind; he had never had a mother; he had not crawled out of a hole in a woman, like other people, like ordinary people, but out of a hole in the ground, like a serpent, and would soon be going back to it.

It was mad, cruel stuff, listened to with an intensity which sometimes turned into fear and outrage. More than once he had to scuttle for safety from the fists and rocks of a crowd he had gathered around him. Later there might come on his face that dismayed look; it was almost as if he were trying to fathom himself, to attend to voices within him which even he had never heard before. But he could not do it; the effort was too great for him; he would abandon it and throw himself into some new trick or folly or piece of criminality. On one occasion he returned to a village which had ejected him and tried to set alight some of the huts in it; he took to springing like a lunatic or common bandit at solitary travellers he came across, shouting, brandishing his knife at them, demanding that they give him everything they carried; in one of his fits of rage he stuck his companion's head into a stream and held it there until the man's struggles themselves became strangely languid or watery, and only then relented to let him go; he announced suddenly that he would neither eat nor drink for three days – and stuck to his word, though he was the one who nearly died on that occasion; he bought a girl in one of the villages he passed through and insisted that you and the little man should be witnesses of what he called his 'marriage' to her, and then sent her away.

How could prankishness and braggadocio be kept out of his fate? It would not have been his without them. He was bound upon ends which were unknowable by him, even accidental, depending on whim and chance, yet ineluctable too. Every attempt to defy them or to escape from them merely brought them closer. The look on his face told you as much.

That look of his began to tell you even more, as the weeks passed. It revealed to you how deep was his suspicion that you were somehow responsible for the change taking place within him. He never said it, he never even hinted at it; to have done so would have been tantamount to making a confession of weakness or anxiety, and that he could not do. Yet you could not doubt that he now felt a special misgiving about your presence, even a sense of threat in it. Perhaps what threatened him was the affection you had for him, in spite of everything; perhaps the silent reproach or appeal which he felt you to be directing towards him; it could have been that for him you had come to represent a longsuffering vulnerability he could not comprehend. But if he was too proud to speak of such matters to you, you were too timid to raise them; just as you were too weak to let him go, too lacking in faith in any possible good your departure might bring about. Besides, what would become of you, where or to whom would you turn?

So you continued together, as before. Then you came to a cluster of habitations which was more town-like than any other you had visited since joining your son in his wanderings. The hill it sprawled over looked at the capital as if from the same height. Between were two lesser peaks and two rough valleys. In this town, or near it, your son lingered. He performed in public there a couple of times, but chose, as usual, to spend his nights outside the town, in one of the valleys below: a region of drab growth, furrowed with water courses, littered with broken terraces and the ruins of ancient settlements, where migrant herders and metal-workers sometimes camped.

You followed him, of course; so did his companion. In a roofless stone shelter that had once been a house you spread out coverings for the night, as you had done so many times before; you built a fire of sticks and fed it with pieces of dried dung; on it you boiled some grains in a skillet, with salt, and cooked eggs simply by placing them in the ashes of the fire. After eating with the others you prepared yourself for sleep. The weather was mild. Stars hung overhead, just where the roof of the hut should have been: so close they seemed.

That night and the night after it passed without incident. So, apparently, did the third. Night-birds uttered their customary calls, jackals howled and cackled in the distance, as if at some kind of special festivity for tormented souls; nearby small creakings, explorings, and scurryings went on constantly. Some of them touched you. The air was still; there was no moon; the stars were steady. Roughnesses and indentations in the ground which you had first felt as a source of discomfort became, as they always did, a part of your body, then you ceased to be aware of them. You slept dreamlessly, waking once to stare into the darkness until you were able to make out broken walls and the spaces between them, the faint glow of the fire, the forms of the others. When you woke again it was near dawn. The stars were dimmer and at a much greater distance than before. The others were gone. Their coverings lay where they had abandoned them.

This did not alarm you. You were sure they would be back. Only after the first rays of the sun had wavered against the sky, then swept across it, and at last struck directly at the nearest hilltop, did you rise. With a small stick you carefully laid bare the orange germ still at the heart of the ashes, and this, with some dry leaves and many puffs of your breath, you eventually succeeded in nurturing into a small flame and a thread of smoke. Out of breath, faintly dizzy, your eyes watering, you continued to sit there patiently, feeding the fire, waiting for the return of the others. They did not come. No one disturbed you. Towards noon you gathered together the belongings scattered around the shelter, hid them in some bushes, and set off for the town.

An unusual silence lay upon it. In the main square, outside the magistrate's court, a small crowd had gathered to gaze at an inconsequential huddle of an object tipped out on the ground. It was the naked body of a soldier. Dusty, complete, contracted, it was dignified only in being forever beyond any shame that exposure might bring. The man's face and brow, fixed in their death-frown, were at a wrong or awkward angle to the skull, which had been shattered at the back by a blow from a stone or club.

All voices, the children's too, were hushed. Even the feet of the townsfolk seemed to whisper as they came into the square or crept away from it. Everyone who approached the body did so with a curiosity that was also a shrinking back. The soldiers on guard stared contemptuously above the heads of the people, or even more contemptuously at them. Some women wept quietly: not in grief for the soldier, but in fear of the punishment that would be visited on them and their menfolk in retribution for his death. The rumour was that the man had been attacked early that morning, while returning from a visit to a woman who lived in one of the gypsy-like encampments outside. Such murders were not uncommon. The hills were full of bandits and zealots. The locals were always held responsible for their acts. It had happened many times before.

Ninth
WH SMITH NOTEBOOK

They took your son and his companion away. They marched them to the capital and you followed. Either you were not noticed, or you were seen and simply disregarded; you did not know which. The men who marched them away were a special group, or seemed so to you: they had heavy buttocks and thick legs and necks, and they eyed one another in such a curious

fashion – each seeking approval from their fellows for everything they did and at the same time provoking or challenging
them to do more, to do better. That is, to do worse. To jerk more
violently at the rope which tied the prisoners together by their
necks; to swear more loudly at them; to laugh more grossly at
their beseeching gestures for food or water.

All this you saw, as an unacknowledged member of the
procession. You left behind the flame-touched, rock-crested,
rock-flanked hills, with black gorges between them, and
plunged at nightfall into the city, with its wide boulevards and
shrinking alleyways, and its own alternations of light and
darkness. Amid some jostling and many averted glances, the
group marched to a street where fewer people were to be seen.
On one side stood a line of thin trees; on the other a long wall
with a pair of wooden gates let into it. In one of these gates a
smaller doorway had been cut.

It opened to a single knock. The men you had been following
were about to disappear through it, perhaps forever. All you
could do so was to rush towards your son and try to touch him.
He gave you his hand, surrendering it to you with a softness
that was unlike him. His friend snorted and whimpered and
shuffled forward for his share of comfort and affection too. He
was so shrunken it was as if you embraced not a body but
merely a strong smell of unwashed skin and woodsmoke. Like a
man confident of what it would bring to him, your son said a
single word: 'Tomorrow.' One by one they bent their heads,

lifted their feet, and passed through the hatchway. It closed behind them.

Tomorrow? The only thing you knew about the tomorrow to which he had made his appeal was that at the end of it the sky would flame up once again, as the earth darkened; and the same would happen again at the end of the following day, and the one after, and the one after that, in an eternity which never wavered, never varied, was never to be penetrated by his will or yours. Time was as hard as the stones under your feet: they were dead, too; nothing would move them; you knew of their presence but they would never know of yours.

Later the moon rose, such a clear, small crescent, the shape of a thumbnail paring, with a few pale stars looking on. You found a kind of shed, where you rested undetected during that night, and then during many of the nights that followed. By day you waited across the street, in the shade of those meagre trees running parallel to the wall. You were not the only one who waited there. Whenever the gates of the hatchway opened, a ragged band of relatives and petitioners drew as close as they dared and peered at the large couryard within; when the gates closed they returned to their places and their abstracted waiting. Everything on this side of the wall, on your side of the wall – trees, street, waiting people – appeared arbitrary, devoid of consequences; on the other side of it, in that unattainable courtyard, every object that could be glimpsed, no matter how briefly, seemed to have a menacing but indecipherable meaning. Everything there was inexorably or mercilessly right: part of a whole, just as it had to be. This was true even of the broken paving-stones in the middle of the yard; of the squeak from the windlass above a well in the corner; of the rolled and knotted bundles of grain-sacks near a stable-block which looked as if they had lain there for years.

None of these, however, was charged with significance to the same degree as the demeanour of the men and women who had access to the place and all it contained. To them it was ordinary! That was how unutterably different they were from the people outside it. To them every day was as unremarkable as every other. They walked about in groups or on their own, spoke to one another, nodded, exchanged documents, smiled, sat on benches or on the ground, yawned, sauntered in different directions; some of the menials even gathered around little fires in the courtyard to cook their food and eat it. All, no matter what their rank, took for granted the entire arena and their presence in it; they even took for granted the beggarly, dispossessed, waiting folk who peered in whenever they were given the opportunity to do so, and approached them timidly when they passed by, and ran at them with written petitions in their hands. Everything normal! Commonplace! Even boring!

And if, sometimes, there were painful scenes at the gates, when new prisoners were brought in, or when condemned prisoners emerged from the courtyard, and they and their relations would tear at each other in what looked like rage but was only despair, or if people cried and fell to the ground, or simply stood there with trembling hands and lips, unable to speak or take a step forward – so what? The underlings, being underlings, had no responsibility for such events; their superiors – people with responsibilities to discharge and careers to nurture – were bound to regard such scenes as simply a part of the job, a reminder of just how much and how little power they had. They were servants of the empire; therefore they were powerful. They were servants of the empire; therefore they were powerless.

So the prisoners would be dragged off, followed only by those they had once belonged to; the noise would die down; the gates would be closed; the remaining supplicants would return to the shade of the trees.

Only once did a prisoner quietly come out through the hatchway, on his own, unheralded, with a stupefied, wary grin on his face: a free man. He scanned the people waiting there; having looked for, and failed to find, a familiar face among them, he made off towards the centre of the city, walking briskly but unsteadily, a man hardly able to believe his own good fortune.

That was how the days passed. Strange days: a kind of unexpected pause or hiatus that had no relief in it. On the contrary, part of the torment. The weather was unpredictable, a mixture of rain and sudden heat; of clear, washed skies and dimmings that could have heralded more storm-clouds or been the first heat-mist of the summer settling on the hills. The little money you had had with you on your arrival was soon exhausted, though you ate hardly at all; thereafter you begged from passers-by whenever you could. Since the street had a bad reputation, relatively few people passed those gates, however, and you were afraid to leave your place, in case something happened while you were away. To the most sympathetic of listeners your misfortune was one to be winced at and forgotten, the plight of a stranger; others just stared or waved you away. You had no idea what was happening inside the building, or even if your son and his friend were in fact still there. You learned nothing from the officials you approached, as they came in and out of that strange territory on the other side of the wall, though you tried to pick out those who looked kinder than others, or readier to talk. None of them had news for you; none of them seemed to know who or what you were asking them about.

Another day. Another moonrise, the moon a little brighter and fatter than it had been before. Another night. Another morning. Once again you learned what you had long known and yet would always find surprising: anticipations of events or misgivings about them never prepared you for what you felt when they actually occurred. These empty days filled up all the space available for them. Like illness or childbirth, they devoured your consciousness of everything but themselves. All that had gone before, from the moment you had met your son, had led up to this, yet little of it seemed to matter now. Then you had been elsewhere; now you were here; that was enough for you to know. Indeed, you hardly had a coherent recollection of just how it was you had come to be in this particular place, on these days among all the others in your life. Random moments from the months you had spent on the road were more vividly, if intermittently, present in your mind, as you squatted silently in the dust, or listlessly answered the occasional question from some fellow-supplicant, than the most recent events. You could remember the look of that dead soldier in the town-square; you could remember also how you had begun to tremble, standing there in the wretched crowd, and how it had seemed to you that your trembling was so violent you were bound to be noticed, and once noticed, assailed. So you had crept away. And then? Go where? And even if your trembling had remained unnoticed by the people around you, what did it reveal to you about your own suspicions or fears?

Somehow you must have made your way back to the place where you had spent the night, though you had no memory of doing so. What followed seemed stranger than any mere lapse or gap in time could be. Approaching the abandoned hut you saw two soldiers sitting at the fire you had made; they sprang up; you ran; they pursued you; you were supine on the ground (had you fallen? had they thrown you down?); they stood over you, laughing. One had a leather helmet on his head, with a strap coming below the chin, and a sword in his hand; the other wore a breastplate, a jerkin, metal greaves, all of which were too big for him. The soldier holding the sword had the face of your son; the other was his friend. How they laughed and showed their teeth. Was this a dream? And if it was not, what was its meaning?

Later a group of townspeople came and captured the two men. Perhaps they had been following you ever since you had crept away from the square. Perhaps by going into town you had undone your companions, and everything that followed was a direct consequence of your action. The men were dragged back to the town, their captors carrying the equipment they had been wearing when you had first seen them. There followed much heated talk and argument among the townsfolk, in the square, while a meeting of the magistrates went on. Would the offering of these captives be enough to propitiate the authorities? At one point someone clapped the stolen helmet sideways on the little man's head; as his hands were tied behind his back he was unable to take it off or pull it straight; it made him look like a one-eyed dog. At another point the people in the square, enraged as much by their secret shame at what they were doing to their fellow-countrymen as by their fear of the authorities, actually tried to attack the prisoners; when the soldiers intervened they turned on them and stones flew in all directions, amid a storm of screams. Nobody knew who was attacking whom and who was defending whom. The prisoners escaped injury, but some men and women were led or carried away with blood starting from their heads and streaking their faces. Almost throughout, even when he was being attacked, your son managed to keep his lips fixed in a faint smile. His companion cried out repeatedly that they had harmed no one; they knew nothing about the soldier; they had come on his equipment in the bushes, where it had been abandoned by someone else. Your son said nothing.

Ancient history, all of it; events that might have been witnessed or experienced by some woman other than the one who was waiting for she knew-not-what to emerge from behind that wall. Just as you had once dreamed of the joy and relief you would feel when you discovered your lost son, now, during this long wait, you developed a new trick or habit of mind: you indulged persistently in fantasies about being discovered by one of the sons you had left at home. He would come walking down this dusty street, quite by chance, and see you sitting there; after a moment of shock and doubt he would lift you gently by the arm and lead you away from this place, to which you would never return. Which you would never have occasion to revisit. Which had nothing to do with you, and never had.

Believing in this deliverance only while you dreamed of it, you remained where you were; so did the wall; behind it, if they were still alive, your son and his friend languished. You did not believe that they had murdered that soldier, though you could not have explained the grounds of your belief. It was of little consequence, anyway. You were sure they would be punished as if they had. Merely to have been found in possession of those items of equipment was enough to damn them, even without the evidence of those who would report the incitements your son had offered against the occupiers of the country. The catastrophe he had been provoking was now upon him. To be found guilty of what he had not done would merely make it so much the more comprehensive.

In any case, almost as if you yourself were the real culprit, you could not get out of your mind the thought that someone had murdered that solider. Someone had picked up a stone or a club and crept up behind him and smashed in his skull. And who knew how many murders the soldier himself may have committed or connived in when he had been capable of it; before he himself had been turned into a victim, into an object? Among all the varieties of pain you felt, therefore, and beyond them, you suffered in the thought of how ready we are to inflict pain on others. Never, but never, had there been a time when volunteers for that task were lacking; never had there been a shortage of occasions or excuses for it. Were it not for that, it seemed to you, everything might somehow be made comprehensible. Even your story and your son's. Even the stars.

Tenth
WH SMITH NOTEBOOK

Only a miracle could save them; and for a few hours, at least, it seemed to you that just such a miracle had occurred. Nor were you the only one who thought so: that was part of the miraculous nature of the event. The sky did not open, the earth did not shake, no voices rose from the ground, no chariot was seen to ascend from earth to sky. But something almost as improbable as any of these did seem to have taken place. The authority holding prisoner your son and his friend and innumerable others, which until then had seemed as immoveable as the hills, as little to be contested as the succession of daybreak and nightfall, as grandiloquently self-assured as the hewn stones of its own public buildings – this authority appeared to totter, it ceased to be sure of itself and at once everything that had maintained it in its place began to erode from within. Its servants, even those of high rank, suddenly looked doubtful and furtive; its soldiers no longer swaggered about the city; the doors to its offices remained closed. In the secrecy and excitement of the moment you managed to find a friend, a woman you had never seen before, a widow, who took you into her house as if you were a member of her family; she was full of a strange certainty, a private knowledge of a kind that was not unfamiliar to you, from other times and other sources, and which you had never set any store by previously. But on this occasion your needs were different and so was your response to what you saw and to what she had to say.

A revolution, it was said, had broken out, or was on the point of breaking out. That was why there was so much shouting in the streets, and so much silence; why thick smoke rose in a column from one quarter of the city and then spread itself in a haze between the entire city and the sun; why soldiers ran or scuttled down empty roadways, sticking close to the walls, their armour creaking and jingling as they ran, like the noise of a horse in harness; why you and your friend climbed on to the flat roof of her house, and lay there on your stomachs, as if you were children playing a game, to peep over the parapet when you thought it safe to do so, without knowing what you were hoping or fearing to see. That was why she talked, with such fervour in her voice and such a devout expression on her face, of the leader, saviour, wonder-worker, a man from your own part of the country, who had entered the capital with his followers and had been greeted by so many people the authorities had not dared to lay a finger on him, but had let him proceed in triumph through the streets. So powerful were he and they, the people together; so irresistible their cause.

In other circumstances, you would have scorned the idea that some group of nobodies, busybodies, provincials, sectarians, fanatics gathered behind an unknown leader, could terrorise both the imperial power and the local administration of priests and policemen who flourished under it. But scepticism was of no use to you now. What else was there for you to hope for? Who else could bring you help? What force could burst open the wall that hid your son from you?

Besides, it was true; everyone was talking of it; those who had been there; those who had heard the noise; those who had heard only the talk of others. The man had come, he had been greeted by jubilant crowds who had uttered wildly seditious cries and hailed him as their king; in spite of all this the authorities had permitted him to leave the city and go back to his place outside it – where, it was rumoured, followers from all parts of the country, but especially from his own northern provinces, were gathering. And that was not all. On the very next day he had actually succeeded in doing again, and doing even more violently than before, what had been remarkable enough the first time. On this occasion he and some of his followers had gone to the temple and in effect raided it, chasing the priests out of their quarters, sending the stallholders and moneychangers flying, setting fire to what they regarded as sacrilegious objects, turning out the imperial soldiery. After carrying out this feat the rebels had once again been allowed by a stupefied and helpless power to leave the city unharmed, untouched, at the moment of their leader's choice.

Now there was only one question to be answered: what was he going to do next, what sign would he now give to the populace? It was rumoured that there were soldiers, not a few of them either, foreigners though they were, who had already gone over to his side. Infallible instructions, it was said, would soon come to him from above. He was about to make a clean sweep of the conquerors. All who had collaborated with them, all who had benefited from their occupation of the land, from the highest to the lowest, would be punished. The kingdom, the true kingdom, would be restored. God's people would come into their own. The blind would see. The lame would walk. The dungeon-gates would open. Some even spoke of the dead rising again. 'Tomorrow,' your son had said. Could it be that he had known something which had been hidden from you? After all, it was no great mistake to have been out in his reckoning – and such a reckoning! – by a few days, or even by a week or two.

Tomorrow? Now not only your son but the whole city was waiting for that tomorrow.

You waited with them. Somewhere, in the city and outside it, decisions were being taken. It was men's business to take them. Your part, the woman's part, was to wait, to be afraid, to be afraid of knowing what you feared; above all, to hope.

Later, hardly more than a day later, came the other tasks that had always been left to women: washing, arranging, wrapping. You had done just those things for him when he was a baby! A thousand times you'd wiped him and washed him and wrapped him in swaddling clothes. Women's work then, women's work now, always women to do such work.

To what end? Only that there should be more of it!

By then it was all over: life, hope, fear itself. What did you have to fear thereafter? It was finished. The miracle had been no miracle; the revolution no revolution; the saviour no saviour; the army of followers no army. A handful of local guards, as zealous as the townsfolk who had captured your son, and as eager to show how loyal they were to their masters, had gone out at night and seized this great leader; and that had been that. They took him only; they did not even bother with the others. In the middle of the night he was tried by the very same priests whom he and his followers had attacked and humiliated in the temple. In the morning he was handed over to the power that sustained them in their position. More men's business: keeping order, weighing consequences, exercising authority first in this direction and then in that; taking what they liked to call the

long view of things. He was a rebel and a trouble-maker. Then
let him be disposed of in the usual way. For misdeeds like his
there was only one punishment. The same was true for the
crimes of which your son and his friend had been found guilty.

Years afterwards, you still did not believe that that which you
had seen with your own eyes had actually taken place. You
knew what had happened, no one could know it better; yet
knowing it, having lived for so long knowing it, was still not
enough to make it credible. The passage of time could do
nothing here. Especially when you were struggling towards or
away from sleep, but not only then, the conviction would
surreptitiously arise in you that some mistake had been made;
that you were labouring under a peculiarly foul and persistent
misapprehension which you would soon be able to banish from
your mind. At such times you would hear voices – sensible-
sounding, rational, quiet, patently veracious voices – telling
you that it could not be that people would behave towards one
another in the manner you had witnessed. It could not be that
someone who had once been your infant, your child, your
growing boy, who had eaten from you and eaten with you,
whose games you could remember, whose fears you had tried
to pacify, whose bedclothes you had straightened, whose hair
you had tied back, whose face you had washed, whose future
you had worried over and tried to envisage, whose disappearance had shattered your life and whose rediscovery had led you
to so much hardship and through so much grief – it could not be
that that person, half-demented wanderer and semi-solitary

though he may have become, could be handed over to other men with skin just as sensitive as his own, bones like his, eyes, hands, nerves the same, hearts thudding perhaps just as rapidly as his, who would torture him until he died. And two more with him! It simply could not be.

So these clear, sensible, never-to-be-stilled voices would assure you. Then you would raise your head from the pillow, or merely open your eyes, and know them to be telling the untruth they had always uttered. That which you did not believe, and could not believe: that alone was the truth.

They opened the big gates early in the morning. You saw your son then, and his companion. They were in the middle of a group of guards, but were no longer bound. There was no need for it now. They could never have run from their escorts; they were too weak from what already had been done to them. Their lacerated backs were bare. Their heads hung to one side. Their eyes were closed.They were jostled into the direction they had to go; they walked without looking where they were going, lurching, staggering, more than once falling to their knees or even sprawling full-length. Then they would be kicked and hauled upright. To those who gathered around the group one of the guards explained laconically, even proudly, 'Bandits . . . . there you are – thieves, bandits.' You heard him. You saw it all. You called to your son but there was so much noise around him your voice was lost. And what could it have done for him if he had heard it? Nothing at all. You were like nothing to him. It was your wish to be nothing to him; if you could bring him no comfort, if you had ceased to exist for him, then the same might be true of the pain he was going through. That was just one of the ideas which swarmed through your mind; or rather, one of the many forms taken by the same, single thought: Let it be quick. Let it be over.

It was not quick. It was not soon over. It took almost the whole day. The atrocity was attended with formalities of all kinds. Afterwards it was easier for you to recollect how these had gone than anything else you saw that day. Yes, they were intended to dignify what was being done, precisely because the important men who had ordained it, and the flunkeys and blackguards who carried it out, were human, too, as human as those they were torturing, and even they, safe in the positions they occupied, bolstered by precedent and law, by orders from above and pressures from below, *knew* what an abomination they were committing. Of course they knew it. But that did nothing to make them relent or turn away or refuse to carry on. Instead they tried to turn themselves into actors in a drama or figures in a tableau – not men responsible for what they did, not creatures with their own motives and feelings. Or if they had feelings, then they were only those which were most dutiful and severe, and therefore least reprehensible. Did they not make manifest the dignity of the state in parading these rags of men through the streets; and then, in due order, handing them over, with the appropriate declarations, to the next arm or organ of authority; and did it not, in its turn, show itself to be of an equivalent or even higher dignity in accepting, after the requisite sealings and stampings, all the obligations placed upon it?

That was how it was done. That was how they hid from themselves what they were doing, even in the very lust and excitement of doing it, and how they managed to enjoy also the forms of these concealments too. There was no end within them to such secret entanglements of pleasure and shame, of display and denial.

Well, your son and his friend were pushed and dragged from their first place of confinement to another public building of an even grander kind, with an open square before it. There they were joined by the leader of yesterday's uprising, who was to go to his death with them. Thorns had been plaited around his head, for some reason you could not understand. All three men were to be flogged again. The man given the task was rehearsing it, making a little twirling run or dance before each stroke, as absorbed as an artist in his work. You fled from the place. They had to go through it; all you could do was flee. Where you found yourself, you did not know. A young woman asked if you were sick and you could not answer her. Later you made your way back to that square. It had to be over by then, you thought; that part of the proceedings could not still be going on.

Indeed, it was over. No one was there. Some dogs were investigating stains on the ground where the men had stood. You did not drive them away. Why should you? They were only doing what it was in their nature to do, like those officials and soldiers and that rapt, dancing man. As you were doing, in that empty square, aware of a continuous female noise, a scream or croak, that could only have been coming from you.

Someone helped you to stand up: until you felt his arms around you you had not known you were lying on the ground. Helping you up was in the nature of this man; so was offering to get you a drink of water from a fountain nearby. You motioned to him that you wanted no water; only to know where they had gone; and he pointed out the way to you.

There was to be no more running away. You stayed to see the rest. Everything. The whole process. Some of it, bits of it, you had not been able to avoid seeing before, back home. Then, now, thenceforward, it roused the same stupid, insistent *They wouldn't!* It isn't true! It can't be true! Nevertheless, they did it. They went about their business. There were signs that the place had been used for this purpose before. The posts were fitted into ready-made holes among the rocks. The operation was a routine one. Some spectators put their hands to their foreheads, to shield their eyes from the glare of the sun. The usual bangings and murmurings arose from the city. All three men suffered the same. When you looked up you could hardly tell them apart from one another; nor could you tell which one of them uttered which cries. Of the throngs who had hailed the rebel and saviour just a few days before there was no sign; now only a small group, easily distinguishable from the random onlookers, remained faithful to him. There were several men among them and two or three women. One of them was his mother. You knew it the moment you looked at her, and she knew who you were. A glance passed between you. It was enough. Words would have added nothing to it. She could not have guessed which of the two men alongside her son was yours; but that did not matter to either of you. They might all have been your sons and hers. Sometime later you were moved to tell one of her companions, in broken phrases, how you had lost your son once before in the capital, all those years before; he seemed to listen; at least he patted your hand. Later still clouds began to come up from the west, as if to meet the declining sun; then the sun mingled with them and sent its rays out at all angles. Strange thoughts came to you. One by one the condemned men would climb down unharmed. You would destroy all who had done this to them. Was it only in your head that someone was calling out 'Mother, mother, mother . . .'? Why did the stones at your feet not know what was happening nearby? How terrible it would be if death were not the end. Only the attentions of the flies, especially those around the eyes and mouths of the victims, and on their lacerated backs, were still irritating them into life, keeping them from death, from rest, from the end of pain. The flies knew what they were doing. It was in their nature.

Then it was over, at last. Hardly any outward change showed that it was the end. Just the dusk and the bystanders beginning to drift away. None of those who remained were sure of what they were permitted to do. Soldiers lowered the posts and tore off the bodies. They carried the posts away for use on future occasions. Your son's body was dry and cold; so was his friend's; no blood came from them now. Despite the thickening dusk everything appeared shrunken and somehow clear. Your son's face was his and yet hardly recognisable; still soft to touch, it was like rock, immitigable, beyond pain. The followers of the other man were preparing a kind of hammock in which to carry him away. The smallest click of stones or catching of a breath came to you from afar. His mother looked at you when they were done, as if wondering how you, being on your own, would manage. It seemed she was about to approach you, but at that point some passers-by came to your help. Apparently they had just arrived at the scene. Using water from a pool nearby, you tried to wipe the bodies with your shawl, and to straighten the racked limbs, and to wrap around them the rags that still hung on them. The hillsides were pitted with caves and old burial places, so the men who had come to your aid had to carry the bodies just a short distance to find a fissure which was large enough to contain them both. When you looked up you saw that everyone in the other party was leaving. Gathered in a close group, they somehow seemed to stand motionless while the darkness advanced on them in irregular jerks or pounces. Even the whitish linen of the hammock was soon reduced to a fragment; then it was gone. Before they left the men helped bring you some earth and stones to cover the bodies. You worked with your bare hands until late that night, adding sand and gravel and branches to what was already there.

Eleventh
WH SMITH NOTEBOOK

What I would like to believe is that you went home after this; that you were received there with more surprise and pity than anger; that you lived for some years with your husband, and for a longer period still, after his death, with one of your sons and his wife, whose children you helped to bring up. You never heard anything again of the man who had died with your son and his friend, or of his mother, and had never an inkling of what they were to become for the world; you never went near the capital again; indeed, you never left your village once you had returned to it.

That's what I would like to believe.

And afterwards –

POSTSCRIPT

There, with an effect of suddenness which may have been deliberate, with one page only used in an otherwise untouched notebook, HER STORY ends. Whether or not Celia Dinan ever intended to continue the tale beyond the point she had reached is for the reader of these notebooks, not their editor, to decide.